Rolling Home

A Pioneer Western Adventure

David Fitz-Gerald

David Fitz-Gerald

Copyright © 2024 by David Fitz-Gerald

All rights reserved.

No portion of this book may be reproduced in any form without written permission from the publisher or author, except as permitted by U.S. copyright law.

Cover design by White Rabbit Arts

Edited by Lindsay Fitzgerald

Welcome

Welcome back!

Ghosts Along the Oregon Trail was written as if it were a single volume rather than a series of five novels. It has been divided into five books which split the Oregon Trail into segments, or legs, of the journey. Readers will enjoy this series most when read in order, beginning with *A Grave Every Mile*.

Howdy friend. Looks like you're going to make it all the way to the fertile valleys we've been fevering to reach. We've been through a lot together, but the worst is yet to come. We couldn't make it without you.

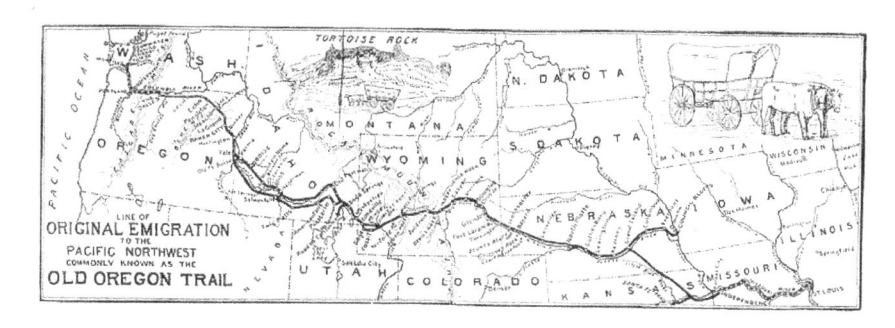

Don't forget, you can find a list of characters online at:

DAVID FITZ-GERALD

https://www.itsoag.com/gatot-cast.

Contents

1. Sunday, September 8 — 1
2. Monday, September 9 — 6
3. Tuesday, September 10 — 11
4. Wednesday, September 11 — 15
5. Thursday, September 12 — 20
6. Friday, September 13 — 25
7. Saturday, September 14 — 33
8. Sunday, September 15 — 53
9. Monday, September 16 — 71
10. Tuesday, September 17 — 76
11. Wednesday, September 18 — 81
12. Thursday, September 19 — 86
13. Friday, September 20 — 91
14. Saturday, September 21 — 96
15. Sunday, September 22 — 102

16.	Monday, September 23	109
17.	Tuesday, September 24	114
18.	Wednesday, September 25	119
19.	Thursday, September 26	124
20.	Friday, September 27	129
21.	Saturday, September 28	135
22.	Sunday, September 29	143
23.	Monday, September 30	147
24.	Tuesday, October 1	152
25.	Wednesday, October 2	156
26.	Thursday, October 3	160
27.	Friday, October 4	165
28.	Saturday, October 5	170
29.	Sunday, October 6	176
30.	Monday, October 7	183
31.	Tuesday, October 8	188
32.	Wednesday, October 9	193
33.	Thursday, October 10	198
34.	Friday, October 11	203
35.	Saturday, October 12	207
36.	Sunday, October 13	211
37.	Monday, October 14	218
38.	Tuesday, October 15	222

39.	Wednesday, October 16	227
40.	Thursday, October 17	232
41.	Friday, October 18	237
42.	Saturday, October 19	242
43.	Sunday, October 20	246
44.	Monday, October 21	250
45.	Tuesday, October 22	261

Sunday, September 8

At Sunday services, Reverend Meadows declines to say a prayer for Snarling Wolf, the man who refused a Christian marriage ceremony. Instead of silently bearing witness to the sermon, I turn my back and walk away from the gathering. I'm not in the mood to worry about eternal damnation today.

I'm drawn toward the unmistakable sound of an axe chopping into wood. Walking slowly gives me time to think about what happened yesterday. It's hard to believe that Snarling Wolf is dead. A wave of guilt floods me. I wished that he would disappear. I tried to deny it, but the man would not let me. He had an uncanny knack for reading my most private thoughts. I wished that he would go away, but I never wanted him dead.

Most of our fellow travelers went to bed late last night. They danced well past sunset, oblivious to the tragic news of Snarling Wolf's murder. This morning, Andrew posted an early issue of the paper. I watched as emigrants read the news. I saw their frowns, hands on cheeks, and wrists on foreheads. It's doubtful that they grieve for the man with whom few interacted. I don't suspect they feel sympathy for his widow. But perhaps now, our fellow travelers will take note of Andrew's warnings.

I tell myself to stop wallowing and do something helpful, so I make my way to the woods. Boss Wheel and the scouts are busy by the river and they don't reject my offer to help. I heft an axe and chop saplings to construct a scaffold like we saw in the Wildcat Hills, near Robidoux Trading Post, over three months ago. I shout, "Timber!" as I drop a slender tree and turn to face Boss Wheel.

He says, "Good work, lady. You got a strong arm. I'll give you that." A faint smile appears despite his thick beard. Giving compliments is not like him. The stubborn old mountain man used to criticize me at every turn. I would never have expected to win over the curmudgeon.

Another straight tree, thick as my forearm, catches my eye. I point at it and ask Ol' Wheel whether I should chop it down.

He says, "That'll do."

When the tree crashes to the ground, I ask Boss Wheel, "Do you think the Lakota will mind being buried in enemy territory?"

"No, I don't think so, Dorcas. His widow says he doesn't mind at all." Boss Wheel chuckles until he begins to cough. "Snarling Wolf befriended our Pawnee scout, which is easy to do, and our Shoshone, which is more of a challenge. Few people can accomplish that."

Boss Wheel guides me with a hand on my shoulder blade. When we reach the glade Rose has chosen, Boss Wheel pulls a toothpick from his pocket and I imagine the taste of pickles. What I wouldn't give for a crisp, sour crunch. Except for carrots, it has been ages since I've enjoyed a vegetable.

Boss Wheel is surprised that Rose knows the customs, and together they preside over Snarling Wolf's funeral. I stand back and away but enjoy the smell of burning sweetgrass. When the ceremony is over, Rose tells me that Snarling Wolf has not *walked on* yet. Instead, he will stay beside her until she reaches Washakie's village. When she has found Sees Through Clouds, then he will join the spirits.

It would be pointless to argue with Rose. I could forbid it, but she would disappear without telling me she's going. Then I would never stop worrying. Perhaps I'll never stop worrying one way or another. Today is not the right time for follow up questions about her planned departure. Maybe I'll feel differently in a couple of years, though I'd be more comfortable if somebody traveled with her. Imagine, letting a thirteen-year-old girl travel alone through the wilderness to go live with Indians she barely knows.

When we reach camp, I'm surprised to see Stillman on his knees scrubbing clothes on the washboard. My eyes search for Dahlia Jane, Christopher, and Andrew as I help Rose settle the few possessions she has back into our wagon. As we are finishing, raised voices at The Hub catch my attention and I step toward the center of the circled wagons.

A familiar argument has been rekindled. Galusha Gains, Samuel Grosvenor, and Horace Blocker argue that we should tarry no longer. Winter is coming fast, and if we don't make our way more quickly, we'll get caught in a snowstorm.

Captain Meadows and The Committee robustly defend their position that without God's blessing, there's no point in going on. The rest of the travelers mill about as if wandering from one side of the argument to the other.

It was easy to ignore the threat of snowstorms when the sun baked our hides in July and August, but we've all noticed the chill in the evening air, hinting that much colder days are on the way. I never thought that I would agree with Gains, Grosvenor, and Blocker about anything, but perhaps we should travel faster than we have been. It isn't just a matter of avoiding snow along the way, we must build shelters to see us through the winter when we get there.

The blaspheming naysayer, Horace Blocker, says, "Captain Meadows, God doesn't care about us. He hasn't from the start. I think He's proven, over and over again, what He thinks of us and our forsaken pilgrimage." Horace lists the names of our deceased and the injuries and illnesses we have suffered along the way.

Captain Meadows' retort reminds us that we can't comprehend God's reasons for the things He does. A couple of travelers grumble in agreement, knowing that we aren't always meant to understand why things happen the way they do.

Before I can stop myself, I find myself saying, "Surely God will forgive worse things than traveling on Sundays."

The men turn to face me and a vote is called. The results show that Captain Meadows' majority is shrinking.

While Sloan and The Radish spy on the travelers, The Viper slinks around the clearing where Snarling Wolf's body perches atop a scaffold. The scavenger plucks the fallen Indian's weapons and fingers the trinkets that flutter in the breeze. The Viper pockets the hairpipe bone necklace, wolf's head charm pendant, and fuzzy hairdrop that the Indian's woman wore.

On his way back to camp, The Viper wonders what to do with the stolen objects. There's no telling what use the extra weaponry could be put to. The stolen trinkets can be displayed in one of his wagons.

Later, as The Viper drifts off to sleep, he imagines an entire wagon decorated with such artifacts.

Monday, September 9

We depart early, as usual, and hotfoot it all day. We skip our mid-day break and take a dry lunch while marching, knowing that we are expected to reach Fort Boise today.

Once the wagons are coiled in their evening loop, a stranger prances into our midst. With his hands at the side of his face, he shouts, "Last chance. Get your provisions here. Last chance before the Blue Mountains. Prepare for the final push to Oregon. Come one, come all, and follow me."

The short-legged man lifts his feet high in the air as he awkwardly trots into a small log building with a modest sign above the door. Just inside the shop, the man greets us with a ready handshake. "Jeremy Bascombe, at your service, but please, call me Remy."

The shopkeeper's face is covered in freckles, many of which overlap. A wide scar divides his right eyebrow, which toughens the look of him. One can't help looking at his broken caterpillar of an eyebrow, despite his strange choice of clothing. Remy's shirt is speckled, his trousers are striped, and his waistcoat is covered in tiny checks. At his neck is a neatly tied, golden-colored string tie. Though oddly combined, his clothes are clean, wrinkle free, and his shirt is tidily tucked in.

"Glad you made it, ladies and gentlemen. Not everybody has been as lucky as you have. Why, just last week, a traveling salesmen told stories of burying a string of bodies along the trail for the last hundred miles. Perhaps you've heard of Muddy George."

Christopher says, "Muddy George, oh yes, we met him at Fort Bridger. That was back on the Fourth of July."

"I declare," says Remy, dramatically. "Anybody who meets Muddy George ain't soon gonna forget him."

Remy doesn't hold back his fearful tales, even knowing that children are present. The young man appears to be in his early to mid-twenties and exhibits childlike qualities himself. I can't help wondering how he ended up a shopkeeper at such a young age. "Some people say there isn't just one gang of outlaws. Listening to the stories everybody tells, it sounds like maybe three or four different gangs now operate along the trail."

Christopher says, "Tell Remy about our stick-up, Mama."

I comply, shortening the story as much as I can. Remy says, "Oh yes, the four horsemen. You're lucky. From what I hear, they steal money and don't kill anybody. But, who knows?"

Cian licks his fingers as he and Oona enter the store.

Remy doesn't proffer his hand but welcomes the Reids warmly, nevertheless. "You look like a hungry man. Can I interest you in some camas roots?" He turns toward the rest of us. "Anybody else? Have you ever tried them? The local Indians think they're a delicacy. Swear by 'em, they do. Who wants a sample?" He turns back to face Cian. "Hold out your hand, pal."

The shopkeeper drops what looks like a small onion into the Irishman's hand.

Cian doesn't need any encouragement. Off-putting as it is to think of eating an onion as if it were an apple, Cian bites into it and makes a contented moan.

Remy says, "Sweet. Crunchy. Pleasant and delicious, wouldn't you say?"

Cian nods.

"Tastes like a pear, don't it?"

Cian nods again.

"Sure, it do. First one's free, then it's five cents a bushel. Load up your wagons, why don't you? You can forage them for yourselves but be careful. Some are delicious. Others are deadly. The Indians know which is which and I know which Indians to buy 'em from. Y'see?"

When Bobby and Wayne step into the store, Remy starts his shtick all over, but the young men nod him off and make their way to a shelf laden with bottles of whiskey. Bobby says, "I'll take one of those."

Wayne says, "Me too. On second thought, gimme two bottles."

Bobby says, "I'd better have three."

Wayne says, "Three then, that ought to get us to Oregon, wouldn't you say?"

Remy repeats the stories so that Bobby and Wayne can hear them.

Bobby says, "That crazy kid is right."

Wayne says, "The newspaper boy, right? Who reads the newspaper?"

I've held my tongue long enough. I'm glad that Andrew isn't here to witness this, but I'm sure Christopher will tell him all about it. "That's my son you bullies are making fun of. What kind of man mocks a child? What if your wives catch you buying overpriced liquor? Three bottles, no less. You can't handle your hooch or your money."

Remy intervenes. "Hey. Hey, lady. What are you doing here?"

To the shopkeeper, I say, "You ain't got to live with these rascals when they've been drinking. I do." To the best of friends, I raise my voice. "Skedaddle, or I'll cluck your heads together again."

Bobby and Wayne scurry away. I can't guard the shop all evening. I'm sure they'll make their way back, but what can I do? A haggard looking man slips through the doorway as they depart. He rubs his chin and tells the shopkeeper, "Just buried another family of four beside the trail. Nothing left of their wagon. Whoever killed dem took everything they had. Wagon tracks lead to the west."

I've had enough. I wish I had not brought Christopher with me. "Come along, son."

Remy shouts, "Hey, lady. You ain't bought nothin' yet. Need some ammunition? Got enough flour? What can I get you?"

"Sorry, sir. We're down to our last twenty dollars and I don't want to spend a cent if I don't have to."

Eight miles to the west of Fort Boise, The Viper runs his fingertips through the fuzz of the hairdrop he pilfered from Snarling Wolf's funerary scaffold. Then, he presses the wolf head pendant into the back of his hand and stares closely at the imprint in his skin until it fades away. He looks at the bone necklace and glides the polished smoothness across his cheek before stowing the stolen trinkets.

When he returns to the small fire, he says, "Our prey has reached the safety of Fort Boise. Soon, we'll do our last job. Then, we retire."

The oldest brother forces a smile, but the thought of leaving the land he loves troubles him. He wonders why he should have to quit. For the thousandth time, he reconsiders retirement. He consoles himself with the thought that he can just as easily unretire, whenever he wishes.

Tuesday, September 10

After a short day of travel, it takes the wagons most of the afternoon to complete their final crossing of the Snake River. It seems that every other wagon's spokes have dried into brittle splinters that break during the crossing. Schuyler Steele and Stillman Southmaid set up a makeshift repair shop and fabricate new wood workings within the wagon rims.

I'd like to think that we've left the worst behind us, but we have been fairly warned. To listen to Remy Bascombe, the shopkeeper at Fort Boise, one might think that every other traveler is murdered on the way to Oregon. However many truly are, it's way too many, for certain, but it can't be fifty percent. How wonderful it would be to roll away from the miserable Snake River, but this crossing is not the last time we will face it. This morning, Boss Wheel said, "We have one more dance with the Snake." We're due to spend our next day of rest at Farewell Bend, but hopefully, we'll vote again and decide to roll away on Sunday morning.

As we wait for the rest of the wagons to traverse the crossing, Andrew sits with his pencil resting on his cheek. He has a pained look on his face. I wish he'd put more cheerful things in the newspaper. Who wants to read vague warnings of impending doom? I chastise myself for my critical thoughts and look at Rose. She sits not far from her brother with her hand resting on her thigh and appears to be staring at her feet. Christopher stands cheerfully beside Scrapple, rubbing the tired ox's neck. I wonder if the thick-skinned creature can even feel the touch of the boy's hand.

It's hard to fathom all the things that have happened since we left Independence, Missouri. What will become of us now? I think of Remy's parting advice. "Keep 'em loaded. If you see a stranger, shoot first and wish them a *how d'ya do*, second. Can't be too careful, ma'am. That's what I always say."

From a small hill north of the emigrants' camp, The Viper crawls through dry grass and pulls a spyglass from his pocket. The outlaw studies his prey, learning as much as he can about them.

As the industrious travelers prepare for another night in unsettled territory, The Viper whispers to his brothers, beside him, "The time is drawing near." A wide grin creeps across his face.

One after another, The Viper describes his future victims, assessing their capabilities and imagining their demise. "That's the trail boss. Drop him first, then the scouts. The Mexican after that. Or the giant. Don't mess with that one. Get a bullet in him fast as you can, he's sure to be dangerous. You can knife the rest. Yell boo at the old one, he'll probably keel over with a heart attack." When The Viper is finished describing the men, he describes the women. "That one looks like a screamer... she looks like she might have the kick of a mule... betcha that one bites."

The Radish pipes in. "Don't kill 'em all, Lennox. Remember, you promised me a pretty young blonde."

The Viper whispers through his teeth. "No, I did not. You promised yourself a pretty young blonde. I promised you a different woman every night this winter. Hold your horses, stallion."

The Radish pictures himself whooping it up with an enthusiastic partner and giggles. "I've been waiting my whole life. I don't think I can wait much longer."

The patient spy maintains his position well into the night, paying close attention to the stock, sharing his wisdom with his companions. "Hey, Radish. They got your horse with them. Didn't think you'd ever see that roan again, did you?"

The Radish is shocked. "Roni? Let me ride in and get her now."

"Don't be an idiot. We'll have all them horses before the week is over. What difference will a couple of days make?"

As the sun begins to set, the night watch commences. The Viper talks as he watches. Whether his brothers wish to or not, they'll be on reconnaissance all night. "One guard sits propped against a cottonwood tree, his hat covering his eyes, and his rifle lies carelessly beyond his reach. Good looking young man. Would a broke a lot of young maidens' hearts." The Viper smiles. "The other sentry seems vigilant, carries a rifle, and has the sense to walk among and around the herd in an irregular pattern, but wears a pink and white dress." The Viper's brow furrows. "They must be desperate to let a woman stand watch. Darned if she isn't the tallest one I ever saw. Better keep our eyes on her too."

After the guard changes at midnight, The Viper watches the transition and then observes the two young men who have the second watch. He kicks his snoring brother in the leg. "Pay attention, Sloan. They're changing the guard. These idiots appear more interested in chattering with each other than protecting the wagon train or the stock. One wears a blue shirt and the other red. One has dark hair and the other is blond." The outlaw's assessment of both men is that neither seems to be a formidable opponent. "Drop either one of 'em with a well-placed fist full a knuckles." The Viper chuckles, "Greenhorns and sodbusters. Easy pickin's."

With a satisfied grunt, The Viper slithers back through the short grass. On the way by, he tugs the pant leg of his sleeping brother and grunts at the other.

When they reach the safety of their hidden camp, The Viper speaks to his horse. "Maybe I will enjoy retirement. Sloan has the right idea. I need to learn to relax and enjoy life. Why not keep my promises? Women are nothing but trouble, but perhaps spending an hour with a painted lady now and then wouldn't be so bad, as long as I don't have to marry one or talk to her, that is." The Viper doesn't know where he plans to take his brothers, but in his imagination, he pictures a big house on a hill overlooking the ocean. But which ocean? What hill?

Wednesday, September 11

It's a long, twenty-mile trudge through Cow Hollow to an arid camp at Keeney Pass. We haven't seen a trickle of water, and after collecting every scrap of wood we encountered, there's barely a couple of combustible handfuls to work with. We shall have to dip into our reserves to heat dinner and boil coffee. If only we could bathe in a refreshing river and shed the thick coat of dust that clings to our skin.

Christopher stomps into camp after visiting Alvah Nye's wagon. He's normally so good natured, but today, he's mad as a hornet. He growls, "They're all dead. All except for one puppy, Mama. That's all that's left. I was supposed to have first choice."

I step back in surprise. "What happened?"

His chin juts forward. "We're not sure. We think they're getting smothered."

"When the wagon moves during the day?"

"Yeah."

"Does that mean you'll be the only one that gets one of Honey's puppies?"

He frowns. "Yeah, I guess so. Why'd they have to go and die?"

I wish I had an explanation to help him. Instead, I say, "It must be tough for Honey to keep still in a moving wagon."

There's a scowl on Christopher's face and I wonder whether he's fighting off tears by channeling anger instead of sadness. "What will we do if something happens to the last one, Mama?" He jams a hand deep into his pocket. "I should carry the puppy myself rather than let it ride in the wagon with Honey." He grinds his ankle into the dirt. "And another thing, Mama. I'm done with this stinking rag. I'm not wearing this blame sling for another minute. I don't care what the doctor says. Hang him for all I care." He sucks a deep breath of dusty air into his lungs and his expression transforms. He says, "Oh, Mama. I got a brilliant idea. I can use the sling to carry the puppy during the day while I drive the oxen. Then, he can spend the night with Honey and Alvah."

Christopher doesn't wait to hear what I think. Instead, he tears off across The Hub toward Alvah Nye's wagon. I'd like to insist that he wear the sling for the full time prescribed, though it is only a few days short. I'm surprised we managed to keep him wearing the sling for this long.

A few minutes later, Christopher runs back, jumping into the air along the way. It's been a long time since I've seen anybody look as free, optimistic, and happy as he looks right now. What a difference from just a short time earlier.

"Guess what, Mama. Alvah says it's a great idea and you know what else? He says he heard that we're three quarters of the way to Oregon. We've only got one quarter left to go."

I shake my head and answer, "Think of that." Truthfully, it feels like we should be a lot closer than three quarters finished by now.

A little more than ten miles to the northwest, Sloan and The Radish argue.

Sloan says, "I'm older, so you should take the stock back."

The Radish's voice raises a couple of octaves. "I did it the last two times. This time, you should go."

The Viper packs tobacco into the bowl of a pipe and scowls at his brothers. He has no intention of letting The Radish take the stolen stock back, but waits until his brothers' argument reaches an impasse. He enjoys it when they bicker, until that moment when he's had enough, loses his patience, and intervenes. Finally, after drawing a few puffs of smoke into his lungs, he barks, "You go, Sloan. Don't waste any time. Meet us at Alkali Springs."

Sloan begins to mount a protest. "But..."

The Viper cuts him off. He leans forward, shoulders bunched, outstretched arm, and finger pointing. His oppressive gaze accompanies his command. Growling, he says, "Go."

Sloan doesn't usually hesitate when The Viper issues an order, but he leans forward and huffs, then turns slowly and scuffles away.

The Viper steps forward quickly and shoves Sloan from his feet with the bottom of his boot on his brother's backside.

Sloan yelps like a dog. "C'mon, man. I'm going. Pshaw!"

The Viper's gaze burns into Sloan's back as his brother leads a chain of stolen stock toward their enclave.

When Sloan is gone, The Viper gestures toward a modest Cottonwood tree near a horseshoe shaped bend in the Malheur River. "Take a break, kid. You've earned it."

When they've settled in the shade, The Radish says, "Tell me about retirement, Lennox."

The Viper grumbles. "Again? We've been over this a million times. Do you really need to hear about it again?"

The Radish chuckles. "It's all I think about. But, no. I don't need to hear it again. I just got some questions is all."

"Oh, you got questions do you? You don't believe me. Is that it?"

"Naw. It's nothin' like that. What I'm curious about is where is retirement? Is it far? How long will it take to get there?"

The Viper answers slowly and starts with a contemplative, "Hm." He turns his head to one side and then to the other. "I ain't decided. We could go to Mexico. I heard of a place called Loreto. We could go to Europe. I like the *sound of Portugal, but that is very far. It'd probably take us a year to get there."*

The Radish says, "We'd better go to Loretta. It sounds closer. Loretta sounds pretty. What's it like there?"

After The Viper tells his brother what he's heard about the coastal Mexican paradise, he places his hat over his head and says that he needs a nap.

The Radish disrobes and makes his way to the river. The water from the hot springs is over a hundred degrees. It's surprising how enjoyable hot water is on a warm day. The Radish searches for the spot where the hot water and cold water meet. When he finds it, he mutters to himself, over and over again. "Loretta, Loretta, the sooner the better." He chuckles to himself, and turns the rhyme into a bawdy song.

Thursday, September 12

After a moderate day of travel, we reach the Malheur River early in the afternoon. Where have I heard that name before? The names of all the rivers, creeks, and swamps run together in my mind, but something about the Malheur sticks out. There's an ominous sound to it.

Then, I remember the whipcord-thin traveler, Larry Pritchard, who rode his cremello into camp one day as I was doing the wash. He had been on his way home to Missouri to tell his mother that her youngest son was dead. An imagined image of Larry's poor brother, Charlie, sticks in my head as I remember Larry telling us that Charlie was killed and scalped by outlaws at Alkali Springs, a day beyond the Malheur. I try to calculate where the downtrodden brother must be now, but cannot figure a guess. Hopefully, he has not starved to death. As a mother, the thought of one of my sons laboring to reach me with the news that the other has been murdered makes me want to keep them both close, and never let them go anywhere.

Men gather at the wagon master's camp. Rose and I linger in a shadow near the corner of our wagon, within earshot. There's widespread grumbling about wasting the afternoon when we could be traveling, but the wagon master insists on staying in camp at the Malheur. We must refresh our water barrels. "We'll not have water for the next two days."

Galusha Gains points to the west and challenges, "We will if we go that way."

Boss Wheel grunts. "Meek's Cutoff? You'll have water for the next couple of days, then a drought after that. What do you know about that trail?"

"It's right here in the guidebook. It says we can skip the Blue Mountains and avoid the Cayuse Indians, if we go this way. If it's good enough for the mountain men, it should do right by us."

"Have you ever traveled that path? Mountain men don't drag along their families and everything they own in heavy wagons."

Galusha snorts. "Of course not."

Boss Wheel coughs, then says, "I've never gone that way either. Everything they say about it spells trouble. We'll stick to the path I know."

It's been weeks since Rose spoke of her imaginary friend. She whispers, "Janey says the enemy is near. She thinks we should take the cutoff, but another spirit says, *Do not go that way.*"

"Another spirit?"

"Her name is Sally. She died here five years ago. Oh, Mama," Rose sniffles. "Sally misses her babies, terrible fierce like."

Flatly, I say, "The spirits don't agree which way we should go and neither do the men."

Rose quakes. "Oh, Mama. Maybe we should just go back."

Andrew and Stillman join us beside the wagon. In a quiet voice, I tell them about the controversy, concluding, "Rose worries about the trail to the west and I'm concerned about the trail to the north."

Andrew says, "I don't have a good feeling about either direction. But, what can we do?"

Rose repeats, "We should just go back."

Her brother challenges, "Home? After coming all this way, you want to go home? That's crazy."

Rose turns her head and says, "No. Just back to Fort Bridger. I don't want to go home anymore, but let's go back to Bridger."

The raging debate in the wagon master's camp is no nearer to consensus than our family meeting. Stillman says, "We should go the way the guides suggest."

Andrew frowns. "Something bad is going to happen. Real bad. I can't figure out what it is or how to stop it. Do you know what Malheur means?" He doesn't wait for anybody to answer before explaining. "It's French for misfortune. And tomorrow is Friday the Thirteenth."

It's not cold, but I shiver anyway. I tell myself that superstitious notions are ridiculous.

After midnight, The Viper and The Radish crawl through the grass, clinging as tightly to the ground as they can, like ants on a tree. When they're close enough to see the sentries, The Viper closes an eye and peeks into his spyglass. "We're in luck. It's the two young men I told you about, Radish: one in a red shirt, the other in blue. They've got their backs to the picket line. They'll never know we were here. See if you can peel away a couple of horses."

The Radish chuckles, but in a hushed tone. "How many we want?"

"Just two for now. I like the big bay, and the black horse on the far end, but you better get the nearest ones instead, just in case the fools catch a lucky break."

"What about my Roni? I want her back. I'll bet I could get away with a bunch more than two."

"No, leave that roan for later. She's been missing this long, another couple of days won't matter none. Understand?"

The Radish grumbles. He knows better than to argue with his oldest brother. He figures waiting a moment will give his brother a chance to change his mind and consent to a more grandiose objective. Finally, he gives up hope and ventures forth on his quest.

The Viper watches as his youngest brother creeps like a wolf toward the horses. The hapless guards are unaware of the horse thief's presence and the horses aren't afraid of the young outlaw. The Radish quietly and gently reassures the horses. Then his fingers make quick work of the knots that tie the exotic skewbald and the black Appaloosa. As the young men assigned to protect the animals and travelers argue, The Radish slowly leads the stolen horses away.

When the outlaws are two miles away from the wagons, The Viper pats his brother's shoulder. The Radish nods in agreement as his brother praises his work. "You ain't much with a knife or gun, but I never saw a better horse thief. Come to think of it, I never saw a more expert cattle rustler either."

Friday, September 13

It's the first thing in the morning. As my feet drop from the back of the wagon onto the dusty ground, Christopher slides into camp. He often doesn't realize how fast he's moving until it's too late, and risks crashing into us. Still half asleep, it dawns on me that he is shouting.

"Why doesn't anybody listen to me, Mama?" It sounds like something Andrew would say, rather than Christopher. "Gwibunzi is gone."

My hearing catches up to me and I holler at him. "What do you mean, Gwibunzi is gone?" My hand reaches for a corner of the wagon to steady myself.

Christopher leans away from me.

"I'm sorry, Christopher. I didn't mean to yell at you." The flash of an image of Gwibunzi kicking Galusha in the head lights up in my head. Is Galusha or Captain Meadows to blame for the mustang's disappearance?

"I know, Mama. The mustang isn't the only horse missing. Coffeepot is gone too."

"Good Heavens, Christopher." I step toward the stones that circle our firepit and lower myself to sit on the ground. I grip my knees and turn back to face my son. "Do you suppose Indians or outlaws got 'em?" My thoughts race, but no matter what scenario I imagine, we're not likely to see either horse again. Losing Gwibunzi feels like losing a part of myself, but what will Dembi Koofai do without the black Appaloosa? How can he do his job without a good horse?

Usually, I'm happy to share anything with a friend, but the thought of offering Blizzard makes me feel possessive. Blizzard normally tosses off anybody but me, but I'm sure the Shoshone scout could manage to stay on the Andalusian stallion. I take a deep breath and force myself to do the right thing. To Christopher, I say, "Would you tell Dembi Koofai that he can use Blizzard whenever he wants?"

The urge to cry threatens to overwhelm me, and Christopher, who is rarely afraid of anything, appears to quiver in fear. I open my mouth to tell him not to worry, but we are interrupted.

Leon Humphries had been passing by carrying a bucket full of water from the Malheur River. He stops for a minute, sets the pail down, and says, "I'm sorry, ma'am. I couldn't help but hear. Did you say horses are missing?"

Christopher answers. "Yes, sir. Two of them. What do you reckon happened to them?"

Leon scratches his chin. "Indians, I'd say. Nothing they like more 'n horses. Wonder who was on watch last night." He looks from Christopher to me, then picks up the pail saying he'd better get a move on.

When he's gone, Christopher says, "Do you think it was Indians, Mama, or do you think it was those outlaws everybody's been talking about?"

I hadn't noticed Andrew's appearance behind me. He says, "It wasn't Indians."

His brother is quick to challenge. "How do you know?"

"I pictured it in my head before it happened. It wasn't Indians."

Christopher's expressive lips twist and he chides his brother. "If you knew it was going to happen, why didn't you warn everybody?"

There's a pained look on Andrew's face. "I didn't realize it would happen so soon."

Who doesn't imagine one dreadful thing or another? Andrew has a way of predicting what will happen. I don't know how he does it. I ask, "If it wasn't Indians, who was it then?"

"I don't know. The image wasn't too clear. There was one man with evil eyes. There was a second man with a small scar near his eyebrow. He was tall and skinny, or maybe his clothes just didn't fit him good. But they certainly were not Indians."

When we stop at noon, a commotion to the east of the trail draws me away from camp and I'm not the only one. As I crest a small hill, I see Oona

Reid, watching a gathering of birds with her jaw hanging open. I salute the vibrant magpies as she has taught me to do.

A winged fellow lays motionless in the dust and a gathering of black and white birds appear as if formally attired, attending a funeral. One bird stands close to its fallen comrade, occasionally nudging it with its beak, as if hoping to encourage it to rise. Nearby, several other birds emit shrill, clicking chirps. A short distance away, another magpie caws. It sounds like a crow.

Oona begins to chant a familiar verse, "One for sorrow, two for joy. Three for a girl, four for a boy, five for silver, six for gold, seven for a secret never to be told."

I've attended enough funerals and I am not in the mood to mourn the passing of a bird today. I turn away, yet Oona's infectious rhyme repeats in my head, unshakeable.

We make our evening camp near a series of putrid holes full of poisonous water. To the west of camp, buzzards circle in the air. Recalling the strange gathering of birds at mid-day, I step from the comfort of our circled wagons and walk a hundred yards from the encampment.

Someone's on their knees, back arched and retching. Realizing that someone is Andrew, my feet speed me to his side.

"Oh, Andrew. Goodness gracious. What's the matter?"

Between heaves, he points in the direction of the circling carrion birds.

Agapito runs toward us, calling, "What is wrong? What is the matter? What is going on?"

Andrew sputters and manages to speak. "It is horrible." He points again to the west and gags.

Agapito's hand confirms his gun is in its holster on his hip and says, "I will see what lies ahead."

Andrew sits back and rubs his temples. I tell him, "Don't move. I'm going to follow Agapito." I tell him I'll be right back and run to catch up to the assistant wagon master.

When I reach him, he turns and holds his hand like Dembi Koofai does for a greeting, but Agapito is trying to keep me away, not welcome me. I disregard his warning and hurry to his side.

The smell of death reaches my nostrils just before the sight of carnage registers in my brain. Then, I hear the familiar bray of a donkey.

Agapito urges, "Go, *estimada. Vete de aquí.*"

I shake my head. The sight is horrible to behold, but I can't back away from it. No wonder Andrew was vomiting. I feel like I might do the same. The body might not be recognizable, but there's no doubt from the surroundings who has been killed. My hand finds my chest. I gag and retch. Somehow, I catch myself. Instead of vomiting, I wail, "Muddy George. It's Muddy George, isn't it? Poor George!"

The robust peddler is staked to the ground. His wrists and ankles are bound to stakes, pounded into the parched dirt. His clothes are gone and not much of his skin remains. His hair has been scraped from his head and chin, and the wild grin that once stretched across his face is replaced with a long, open mouth and a wide-eyed terror. Despite the hopelessness of his situation, it appears that the man died fighting and screaming. The fact that his skin has been peeled from his face makes the scene even more gruesome.

Turning partially away, I rest my forehead on Agapito's nearest shoulder and he stretches a comforting arm around my back. With his other hand, he attempts to cover my eyes, but it is too late. I could not forget having seen this. The peddler's cart has been smashed, his wares blow across the desert, and three dead donkeys are mourned by a braying companion. There's a dozen arrows in each of the fallen beasts. Muddy George's precious banjo has a punctured head, snapped neck, and severed gut strings.

With a sniffle, I pull away from Agapito and step toward the orphaned, fourth donkey.

Agapito tries to stop me. "Me and the scouts, we will take care of Muddy George, *estimada*."

I return to his side and rest my cheek against his, facing away from the carnage. Then I sniffle again and retrieve the surviving burro.

Andrew is just climbing to his feet when we make our way back to him. He holds his stomach and says, "Why doesn't anybody listen to me, Mama?"

That's the same thing Christopher said this morning when he told me that the horses were stolen.

He slumps and his expression matches his posture. "I keep warning everybody."

"I know you do, dear, and everybody is wary. What more can we do?" I wish we could have saved the charismatic huckster, but how? When we last saw Muddy George, we had just departed Fort Bridger. With a hand in the baggy pocket of my trousers, I palm the mane comb and flip it over and over again.

Almost two hours after midnight, The Viper and his brothers crawl on their bellies across the chalky ground, getting as close to the travelers' stock as possible. The Viper turns a dill flavored toothpick between his lips. He thinks, How clever of the peddler to make them taste like pickles.

Sloan whispers, "Why can't we steal their cattle after *we kill them. What's the point of doing it now?"*

The Viper shushes his brother. He has no intention of justifying the plan in the middle of executing it. Instead, he reports, "They have three on watch tonight and one of them is that woman."

The Radish says, "Oh good. Let's take her instead of the cattle."

"No. That's not good. She's twice as diligent as any of the other guards."

When it comes to the subject of women, The Radish is not one to give up easily. "All the more reason to take her, wouldn't you say?"

"No." The Viper hisses. "She'd scream loud enough to wake the dead peddler and his donkeys."

When they get close enough, The Viper says, "Remember the plan. I'll throw the rock. When they run toward the sound, cut those yearlings loose and drive them home."

Saturday, September 14

The boys walk with the wagon during our daily march, and I do my best to console Cobb. He had such high hopes of running a fine herd of Devons in Oregon. When I spy the wide river in the distance, I leave Cobb with his wagon. Walking away, I feel disheartened. How can I help Cobb when there's nothing I can do? There's no chance of him getting his yearlings back. I think of Gwibunzi and Dembi Koofai's precious Coffeepot—gone forever.

Upon arrival at Farewell Bend, our last encounter with the Snake River, we water the stock and replenish our barrels. After a seventeen mile march across a parched land, the fertile stripe of riverside refreshes our spirits a bit, but firewood is scarce. We collect what little we can find and combine our efforts, making a shared fire near The Hub.

After settling in, I stand beside the river with Christopher and Dahlia Jane, looking about for a place to bathe. Christopher says, "Look at that island. I want to swim over to it. Can I, Mama?"

Before I can answer, Andrew runs toward us, shouting. "Rose has been taken." He points a shaking hand toward the south along the riverbank.

"A skinny man on a brown horse with a floppy hat——I saw it, Mama. We must follow them."

"Hurry, Andrew. Let's get help." I pluck Dahlia Jane from the ground and run behind Andrew and Christopher, back to the wagons. Andrew breathlessly tells Agapito what happened as I hand Dahlia Jane to Stillman.

The assistant wagon master sends Arikta along the trail to the northwest where Boss Wheel watches over the camp from a short distance away. Then, Agapito says, "I do not know where our other scout is, *estimada*. Try not to worry."

Agapito's words are not encouraging. When Boss Wheel returns, he listens without dismounting as Andrew describes the kidnapping. Andrew points to the south. "They went that way. You gotta save Rose."

The man who reportedly misses nothing, and sees all, failed to notice Rose's abduction. Boss Wheel says to me, "You stay here," and to Arikta, he says, "and you come with me." Then, Boss Wheel turns back to me. "It's always that same girl, isn't it? Sometimes I think she is going to be the death of me."

We watch as Boss Wheel and Arikta's horses gallop along the bank of the Snake River to the south. When I can't see them anymore, I turn toward Agapito. Despite my attempt to control my emotions, my lip quivers. I'm not a woman who cries very often, and rarely out of sadness, but sometimes due to anger or fear. Losing Gwibunzi was one thing, but now, Rose has been taken. My heart races and I think of the outlaws that everyone can't stop fearing.

This is no time for tears.

Agapito steps forward and wraps his arms around me. My body shakes as I hyperventilate. Andrew's dire warnings repeat in my head and all I can think of is that the worst possible thing will happen. If we don't get to her, Rose will be doomed. We must try to save her.

When Dahlia Jane's arms clutch my thigh, I freeze. My shaking stops. My children need me. I pull away from Agapito, thank him for comforting me, and tell him that we will return to our wagon.

It strikes me that he's trying to muster a reassuring tone. He says, "Let me know if you need anything, *estimada*." Then, Agapito looks at Andrew and says, "Keep calm and help your Mama. I will check on you in a little while, yes?"

When we reach the wagon, I whisper into Stillman's ear. "I have to find her. Don't tell anyone until you must. Watch the children while I slip out of camp."

Dahlia Jane and Christopher listen as Andrew tells Stillman the extended version of witnessing Rose's abduction. I take small steps back and away from them, quietly lift my saddle from the ground, and inch toward the picket line.

I start riding at a walk, hoping nobody notices my departure until I can no longer restrain myself. I'm sure they can still see me from camp, if they're watching, but I squeeze my legs together, sending Blizzard into a gallop.

After a couple of miles, the Snake turns sharply toward the northeast. Other than following the riverbanks, I don't know what to seek. I decide to rely on intuition, chance, or supernatural guidance, as do Rose and Andrew. When the river turns toward the southeast again, Blizzard plunges into the water. After fording, we follow a narrow stream that trickles into the Snake River, heading away from the infamous waterway.

With a tug on the reins, I pull Blizzard to a stop and close my eyes. What does it feel like when Andrew gets a premonition or Rose is about to communicate with the dead? Hoping to receive some sort of otherworldly signal, we sit and wait. Nothing happens. A sense of hopelessness weighs heavy on my sagging shoulders. What chance do we have of finding Rose? Probably none. What direction should we look? If only I could track and read trails, like Arikta and Dembi Koofai.

I mutter, "Maybe you have more sense than I do, Blizzard." I relax my legs, loosen my hold on the reins, and let him have his head so that he can set our course. The horse walks slowly along the small creek as it trickles east, then turns northward.

A mile along, the creek ascends into a canyon between steep, barren hills. There is no sign that anyone has followed this path, at least no tracks that I can recognize. Blizzard tenses as I take control of the reins again. He tosses his head in protest and I steer him back along the creek. We should return to camp.

A voice calls out, "Freeze. Hands up. Reach for the sky."

I gulp and Blizzard turns back toward the north.

A lanky young man stands behind a boulder and shouts. "Git off that horse." The kid looks just like Andrew's description of the man who abducted Rose.

In a voice that is so gruff, I amaze myself, I challenge, "Who are you?"

He tips his head back, looks down along his nose at me and says, "I'm The Radish. Who are you?"

With my hands still in the air, I say, "My name is Dorcas and I'm looking for my daughter, a girl in a dark purple dress. Her name is Rose. Have you seen her?" A thought rattles in my head. Where have I heard 'The Radish' before?

"Oh yeah, I seen her. First girl I seen in half a year, at least." The boy laughs like he's thinking unwholesome thoughts. His hands grip the oversized buckle on his gun belt, and he jostles it.

Crossly, I say, "She's my daughter and I must find her, Mr. Radish."

The man guffaws and slaps his knee. "It's just Radish, lady, or The Radish, not Mr. Radish." Does his name have something to do with his rosy-red cheeks, or is he blushing? There's a small, crescent moon-shaped scar above his eyebrow.

"Can you take me to her? And can I lower my hands?" Without waiting for a response, I begin lowering my arms.

The Radish glances at the rifle on my saddle, saunters over, and says, "I reckon I'm gonna hafta." He plucks the revolver from my holster and stows it in my saddlebag. I'm astonished when The Radish vaults from the ground without taking a running leap and lands behind me. My skin crawls when he places his hands on my hips.

He says, "Follow Hog Creek to the north."

The young outlaw draws shallow breaths, heating my neck. I can picture the ruddy-gilled knave panting like a wolf behind me as he presses into me.

In short breaths, he says, "I ain't never been with a woman. You can be the first." His shaky hands slide forward and up. When he gropes me, I elbow him hard. He laughs and says, "The Viper is going to take me to a bordello this winter."

I want to tell the boy to keep his mitts off me, but his words distract me. "The Viper?"

"My brother, Lennox. We call him The Viper."

"So there are two of you?"

"No, there's four of us. The Viper, Leon, Sloan, and me. We're *outlaws* and we're gonna be rich." The way he says outlaws makes him sound like he's in awe of himself and his brothers. Then he seems to change his tune. He quickly adds, "But I don't care about being an outlaw." His hands return to my side.

"What do you care about?"

"I told you already. Women. I just want the *women*." His hands travel from my waist along my thighs as his chest presses into my back.

I grab his hands and squeeze them so tightly that he yips like a dog when somebody steps on its tail. "I am not that kind of woman, Radish."

He laughs. "I don't care. I want all kinds of women." Again, his hands reach around me, only this time over my arms, and he roughly palms my breasts. He adds, "Maybe a hundred different women."

This time, my elbows smash into The Radish's ribs. "Knock it off."

"All right, if you say so." The boy slides from the horse, pulls my rifle from its scabbard, and points to the left. "Ride into that draw."

Instead of letting me proceed as instructed, The Radish guides Blizzard with a tight grip where the bridle meets the bit. A hundred yards in, there is an entrance to a cave. Looking more closely, I see disturbed soil. Piles of discarded rocks and pebbles dot the hillside. Have they got Rose hidden in a gold mine?

A scruffy-looking man with piercing blue eyes emerges from the cave. A cigarette hangs from his lip, and he grunts. I dismount and whisper to the Radish, "Is that The Viper?"

"Yup," he says. Then, he speaks to his brother. "Look what I found. Can I have her?"

I turn, slap the Radish's face, and caution him to mind his manners. Then, I speak to his brother. "I am Dorcas, and I'm looking for my daughter, Rose." There's a burning sensation in the back of my throat. I look around quickly, not just for Rose but also in consideration of potential escape routes.

"I see." The Viper stands, staring at me, apparently in no hurry to say or do anything. His hypnotic gaze bores into my eyes, reminding me of Armand Bartholomieux. The Viper speaks to his younger brother through his teeth. "She alone?"

My legs begin to shake and I feel dizzy. The look in The Viper's eyes is most disturbing. If only he'd look away. I wish that I could flee, but I can't leave Rose. Where is she?

The Radish casually jams his hands into his pockets. "Yup. I didn't see anybody else." He laughs as his eyes travel up and down my body. "Foolish woman. Just my type."

"Quiet!" The Viper admonishes his brother. "Every woman is just your type. You don't know what you're talking about. Women are nothing but trouble, don't you remember?"

The Radish frowns and says, "C'mon, Viper, that was just Ma, not all women. And besides, that was a long time ago."

"Hush. We've got a job to do. Focus on *that*, and like I promised, you'll have more women than you can handle, come winter. Pretty young women, not old dames like this one here."

From inside the mountain, I can hear Rose's voice. "Mama! Is that you? I'm in here." Abandoning Blizzard and ignoring the outlaws, I run toward the dark opening, calling my daughter's name.

Just inside, the ground slopes slightly downward and to the right. A fire's glow illuminates a small area and ropes bind Rose's ankles and wrists. Nearby, another man slouches against the wall of the cave. Without getting up, he says, "Howdy, ma'am," as if he anticipated my arrival.

The Viper has followed me in. He barks an order, "Tie her up, Sloan."

The man groans as he sluggishly climbs to his feet, reaches for a stretch of rope, and approaches me. "You heard the man. Hands behind your back, lady." Sloan doesn't put much effort into binding my hands.

Sloan grunts and nods his head toward Rose. "It'll be easier on ya if you sit down before I tie yer ankles." I sit beside Rose and give her a look that I hope she finds reassuring, but she has not acknowledged my arrival. Instead, she sits with a slouched posture and gazes intently into the darkness of the cave. Does she realize how dangerous this situation is? Once again, it appears that her mind has wandered away. When my legs stretch out before me, Sloan sighs, drops to a squatting position, and binds my feet.

It could be ten minutes or it could be an hour. It's hard to account for time when one is held against their will. The brothers move about the cave and I study their interactions. Rose barely moves. Maybe she finds it comforting to retreat within herself. The Radish and The Viper seem to know their way around the place and I wonder how much time they spend here. This can't be their home.

Is it better to try and be invisible? There's no chance that the outlaws will forget we are here. Finally, I decide to speak to them. The Viper turns toward me when I shout out, "There must be a dozen men out looking for us."

He says, "So what?"

I add, "Some of them are Indians, and they're very good at tracking, you know."

The outlaw tells me to shut up—not in a way that reveals concern, but rather in a way that conveys no wish to continue our conversation.

There's a commotion as two men shout at each other near the cave's entrance. I'm surprised to hear Boss Wheel swearing, and even more so when I realize that the other man's voice belongs to Leon Humphries. What is he doing here? I thought that Arikta had accompanied Boss Wheel.

When I challenged The Viper, I was trying to make him doubt himself. I didn't actually believe that we'd be found.

I shimmy around and watch as Leon Humphries hugs The Viper like a long-lost relative. My head bobs, my jaw hits my chest, and I gape at the encounter. Then, I remember The Radish said that his brothers were named Lennox, Leon, and Sloan. I gulp and whisper to Rose, "The enemy has been among us the whole time—ever since we left Independence." Then, I remember him watching when Larkin's safe was discarded. How many times did I see the man watching people, and standing near people's wagons without any reason for being there?

Recalling that Boss Wheel departed with our Pawnee scout, a question comes to mind. What happened to Arikta? Maybe they split up to cover more ground.

The Radish slaps his brother on the shoulder. "Welcome home, Leon. Good to have you back home." Then The Radish raises his eyebrows at me suggestively as he roughly escorts Boss Wheel toward us.

Sloan passes the extra rope to The Radish, and greets Leon enthusiastically. My voice finds me, and I blurt, "Mr. Humphries! *You* are the outlaw's brother?"

Leon tips his head back and laughs. He sounds proud of himself, and now I can see that he resembles his youngest sibling. "Yes, only the name is Leon McAdams, not Humphries."

The Radish's head bobs as he chuckles. "You really had the pilgrims fooled, didn't you, Leon?"

Quick to the point, and back to business, The Viper waves his brother to his side and asks, "What do you know, Leon?"

Leon frowns. "I'm not sure we picked a good target. Maybe it's worth a few bucks. This 'un here, Dorcas Moon, was traveling with a big heavy safe, but when she dumped it along the Platte, she opened it in front of everyone, and there wasn't a thing in it."

The Viper says, "Why carry an empty safe? They must have money somewhere in their wagon."

Leon shrugs. "I searched their belongings a couple of times. I couldn't find anything. Maybe she carries it with her. She wears a man's trousers under her dress, and," he pauses, waves his hands about my bosom, and continues, "maybe she's got something hidden under there."

"Mr. Humphries," I gasp. "Good Heavens! I can assure you that I am not carrying a single dollar on me. Furthermore, we spent our whole life's savings outfitting ourselves for this trip. The safe was an investment, so that my husband could establish a bank when we reached Oregon, but we're broke. We have got nothing left."

Leon turns to his brother. "I don't believe her. They must have money hidden somewhere. I just haven't found it yet."

"Mr. Viper, I can assure you, we are not worth robbing. And I can vouch for our friends, also. None of us are wealthy."

Ignoring me, The Viper asks his brother, "What about the rest of the wagons?"

"There's a pair of spinsters traveling with a teenager. Got a wagonload of gems and jewelry. The captain carries an expensive watch, but I haven't been able to search his wagon. The doctor must have money. Other than that, I think the wagon master has all the cash. I haven't found a cash box in his wagon. I think he carries it all on his person."

The Radish hasn't succeeded in binding Boss Wheel's wrists and ankles.

The Viper snaps off an order. "Take his coat and vest. Search him good before you tie him up."

Boss Wheel curses and protectively clings to his garments as the outlaw tries to separate him from his capote.

Like a pack of wolves, the brothers descend on the furious wagon master, knocking his hat off of his head. The former mountain man growls like a grizzly bear, hacks a cough, and hurls a wad of phlegm into The Viper's face.

The Viper hisses, "Step back." He snaps his pistol from its holster and points it at Boss Wheel. Leon, Sloan, and The Radish back off a couple of paces. Without blinking, The Viper says, "You're going to regret doing that." Boss Wheel's spittle drips from The Viper's face.

Nobody moves, and the cave is silent. Boss Wheel sneers at The Viper. The Viper's evil stare looks like it could melt a hole in Boss Wheel's forehead.

Boss Wheel hacks up another throatful of phlegm.

The Viper growls, "Nobody spits on me."

The former mountain man takes a deep breath, clearly intending to defy the notorious outlaw.

The Viper squeezes the trigger, plugs Boss Wheel from close range, blowing a fat hole through his chest. Through mashed teeth, The Viper says, "You ain't gonna do that again." He wipes mucus from his face with his sleeve while Boss Wheel crashes to the ground. Then, The Viper turns to Leon and says, "Now search him."

Rose and I watch in horror as the brothers descend on Boss Wheel, rolling his body to the side, confirming that his injury is fatal. Why didn't he fight back? Instead of humiliating the outlaw, why didn't he charge? Though I hate it when men fight, I wish that Boss Wheel had attacked The Viper. If he had, maybe our luck would have changed.

My memories of the man flash through my mind as he draws his dying breath. I remember standing beside him at his favorite place. What did he call it? Thousand Springs? He said that was the landmark that kept him coming back, year after year. He said that he never felt more alive than when he was near the glorious, cascading waterfalls. To think, when we started our journey, I resented this grouchy old loner. Somewhere along the way, he grew on me. Now that he's gone, all I can think of is how pointless his murder is.

Like vultures on carrion, the brothers strip Boss Wheel of his capote and his waistcoat. I remember the day that I saw him washing his long trapper's coat in the river.

The Viper is impressed by the weight of Boss Wheel's garment. He tells his brothers, "The old goat must be carrying every dollar he ever made. If only everyone did. It would make our work much easier. We'd be filthy, stinking rich."

I can't help staring as they rip Boss Wheel's clothes to shreds, liberating a fortune from too many hidden pockets and secret compartments to count. They've amassed an impressive stack of banknotes and a tall pile of Seated Liberty dollars at the dead man's feet. It is a wonder Boss Wheel could haul so much treasure with him everywhere he went.

The Radish picks a shiny coin from the pile, holds it toward the firelight, and runs his fingertip across its surface. He looks at me, and says, "You look just like the lady on the coin." He laughs, and the sound reminds me of Muddy George's braying donkey.

Rose has a vacant expression on her face, the one that makes me fear for her sanity. The one that she gets when she claims to see dead people. Perhaps she imagines she can hear Boss Wheel, and I wonder if he's more talkative as an apparition than he was as a man. I close my eyes and shake my head. Good Heavens, am I starting to believe that dead people talk to Rose?

Turning back to face the brothers, and watching them paw over Boss Wheel's fortune, I'm overwhelmed with anger at their greed. If I thought that I could spit on them without getting shot, I'd follow Boss Wheel's lead. Instead, I muster all the disgust I can and spit out my words, "You killed this man for *that*?"

The Viper smiles at me, baring his teeth like he plans to bite me. "I'd kill him five times for half as much. *That* will take care of my brothers and me for a couple of years. When we search your wagons and sell your stock, we will be set for life."

Rose looks at The Viper and speaks. If she's afraid, it doesn't show. How does she remain so calm? In a strong voice, she says, "Olivia doesn't want you to kill anybody else."

The Viper stands quickly, and his brothers look away from the horde. The Viper says to Rose, "What did you say?" It is as if she has scraped against a wound. She has certainly gotten his attention.

Rose draws a slow breath and speaks as if she's told the outlaw, hundreds of times, "Dead people speak to me. Your sister is here. She understands why you killed your mother and father, and she forgives you for accidentally shooting her, but she wants you to stop robbing and killing people. Now."

The Viper drops to a squat beside Rose. He sneers, "What kind of trick is this? I should kill you and your mother both—and be done with you." Inches from Rose's face, he stares at her as if he's trying to cast a spell on her with his eyes.

Undaunted, she says, flippantly, "But you won't because your father told me where he hid the money."

The Viper twists away from Rose, looks at Leon, then Sloan. Blinking like mad, he says, "That girl is crazy. Like some kind of demon. I don't want to hear another word. Gag her."

Bravely, Rose says, "Let everyone go, and I'll tell you where to find the money your father stole when he robbed the bank in Sullivan."

The Viper slowly rises to his feet. "Sullivan? Sullivan, Missouri." From the tone of his voice, he sounds astonished. "How can you possibly know about that?"

A deep, familiar voice surprises the outlaws from the mouth of the cave. "Hands up. We got you surrounded."

The Viper turns, draws, and shoots into the darkness.

An unseen body drops to the ground with an audible thud, moaning.

Three shots are fired from near the mouth of the cave. In brief flashes of light, I can see Alvah Nye, Dembi Koofai, and Arikta.

The Radish scrambles for his gun as The Viper fires again. When Leon fires, I see Alvah hastily dragging a body through the mine's entrance. Then it is quiet. A few minutes later, I hear the beat of horses' hooves as those who attempted to rescue us retreat. *Who was shot?*

I look from one brother to the next, and lastly at Sloan, who holds his hand on his side. He groans and rips his shirt off. "I been hit."

The Viper points with his gun, "Radish! Check his wound. How does it look?"

After a quick examination, the youngest brother says, "Sloan's gonna be fine. They gouged a little chunk of meat off him, though."

The Viper barks, "Fix him up, then stand guard at the mouth of the cave. Leon, fetch our horses."

On the way to Farewell Bend, Leon tells his brother everything he knows about the assistant wagon master, scouts, and passengers. The Viper looks at the circled wagons from a distant hill through a spyglass, and Leon answers question after question.

With their survey completed, The Viper announces his plan. "I'll create a diversion. You scatter the horses. When you hear gunfire, drive the nags off."

Without waiting for his brother's agreement, The Viper rides Boss Wheel's horse to within a couple hundred yards from the circled wagons.

Stillman returns from the Snake River carrying a bucket of water in each hand and nods a greeting at Garland while passing the Knox's wagon. Garland makes his way toward the riverbank. Stillman turns his head and looks directly at The Viper, drops his buckets, looks away, and shouts into camp, "Attack. We're under attack."

Stillman drops to the ground a split second before The Viper's rifle fires in his direction. His heart pounds. His eyes blink rapidly, and he whispers to himself, "What just happened?"

Clipper pivots. The Viper grabs the back of Garland's shirt and yanks him up into the saddle in front of him. The outlaw gallops away with his third captive as Stillman rolls from his back to a kneeling position, and then stands, legs wobbling. When he regains his feet, he looks around and sees a woman on the ground nearby. His hand slowly covers his mouth. It should be him, dead on the ground, not her. The bullet meant for Stillman has instead found Hannah Knox.

The dying woman's body twitches while Miranda rushes to her side and drops to her knees beside her sister.

Sloan moans in agony with his hand pressed against a crude bandage.

The Radish's stomach growls so loudly that it makes me hungry. I try to avoid looking at Boss Wheel's corpse.

"Radish, untie me, and I'll fix dinner. I'm a pretty good cook."

"That's good because Sloan does all the cooking around here. But he's lazy. All he makes are beans and biscuits."

"What do you have?"

The Radish unties me, and after examining their scant provisions, I say, "I'm sorry Radish. With these provisions, beans and biscuits are all I *can* make."

"Git to it then." He smiles at me obscenely. He lustfully gropes his big belt buckle like he's wondering whether he should try to get away with something while The Viper is away.

I warn him. "Don't even think about it."

He flashes me a half-smile and grips his chest like he's been shot. "It pains me that you don't want me. Think of the fun we could have." He glances at Rose, then back at me. "I bet you could show me a thing or two." He laughs and stands a short distance away, pointing his gun at me while watching me prepare supper. "Make enough for Leon and The Viper while you're at it."

My mind races. If only I could poison them. Having to cook for them feels like taking care of them, yet I'm glad to be busy doing something. I'm tempted to attack The Radish. I try to calculate my odds. Ultimately, I decide not to make our situation worse.

After eating, The Radish ties my wrists and ankles, and then he fondles me again. I roll away into a ball and insult him mercilessly. My words echo in the cave. My tirade only excites him more, and I flop about trying to escape from his lewd caresses as Rose kicks and tries to trip him with her bound legs.

When The Viper growls from the mouth of the cave, The Radish jumps to his feet. I don't know why The Viper doesn't let his little brother have his way with me, but that's about the only thing to be thankful for at the moment.

The Radish retreats to the cave's wall and leans against it. The Viper throws Garland Knox to the ground. He says to the boy, "If you know what's good for you, don't move a muscle."

The outlaw squats beside Rose, and she again explains that she can communicate with the dead. The Viper must have been thinking about what Rose said earlier, while he was away, and it seems that he now believes her. "You and your family will have to travel back to Missouri with us."

"Only if you let everyone go. Otherwise, I will not tell you. I will not show you. Besides, if you don't stop killing people, the ghosts will haunt you and make your life miserable."

The Viper seems to consider what Rose says. He says, "We'll see. In the morning, we shall see."

A quiet settles over us. I can't imagine falling asleep, given the danger we're in and the discomfort of my bonds. Nobody has bothered to remove Boss Wheel's dead body.

Silently, I fume. Outlaws want to rob me of my future, kill my family and friends, and destroy our dreams. We spent our entire life savings on this trip, and I cannot let this happen. I am a wild mustang. This pack of wolves can not hurt me. Tomorrow, they'll see that they messed with the wrong woman.

Finally, sleep provides escape from the outlaws.

Sunday, September 15

I awaken before dawn. Something moves against my leg. My first thought is of The Radish, but whatever touches my limb, it is not the hand of a man.

My jaw clenches, and I open my eyes, but not much is visible in the dim light of a wasted fire. Blood courses through my body, and my heart thunders in my chest as a thick snake twists across my lap.

Sweat covers my body. My wrists are tied together and rest on my stomach. The heavy weight of the giant snake seems to have settled on my abdomen. Remaining still takes all the courage I can muster.

The writhing beast's head appears above my trembling fingers, then wraps a coil around my hands. The rest of its length follows the head and slithers about my bosom. The restless creature ceases its movement. Its arrow tip shaped head rises. The snake's skin has a diamond-shaped pattern, and its grayish-white eyes remind me of Washakie's medicine man, Sees Through Clouds. The reptile's tongue darts in and out of its mouth, inches from my face. My mouth is dry, and I can't help blinking hard. From somewhere

I can't see, the serpent shakes its rattles, confirming its identity. This is a rattlesnake.

I can't help thinking that there is something more to the snake than reason can explain. The intimate nature of its exploration of my body makes me wonder. Is there something about me that compels its presence? Does it like or despise me? The serpent wags its head near my chin. It takes all of my willpower not to roll away and scream. Any second, it could flip its jaw and strike me with its venomous fangs.

After what seems like hours, the snake's head curves and its body follows, traveling from my shoulder and down along my arm. It crosses my belly, winds past my bound wrists, then slithers along my legs, finally scraping itself slowly against the rough surface of my worn-out boots.

Finally, the serpent is gone, and my tense body goes limp. Just as I begin to gather my wits, a screaming man barrels through the mouth of the cave. It takes me a moment to realize that it is The Radish. He shouts. "They're upon us. We're under attack again."

Shouting voices from beyond the mine's entrance confirm The Radish's warning, but I can't make out who is there or what they're saying. Did the outlaws believe our fellow travelers would give up on us? Did The Viper think that without Boss Wheel's leadership, our friends would abandon us? I worry. If they have come to rescue us, what chance do they have? From the dim cave, picking off anybody that appears at the threshold should be easy.

Despite the commotion, I glance about and notice a coiled rope beside the fire, merely a couple of feet away. I sit forward and tip my head to get a better look. There's a bulky weight in my dress pocket that I hadn't noticed.

Maybe it was because of the frightful presence of the rattler that I didn't notice it sooner. With my forearm, I press against the object. Could it be a revolver? How could a gun appear from out of nowhere? Then I realize that the rope at my wrists has loosened.

Several men flood the entrance as The Radish's groggy brothers leap from their blankets. They scramble to grab their weapons and ready themselves for whatever is coming.

With their attention focused on the entrance to the cave, they don't notice when I slip my wrists from the rope, freeing my hands. I blink rapidly, keeping pace with my thundering heartbeat. My hands confirm the shape of the object in my pocket. It is in fact a revolver.

Our rescuers dive into the cave and fire in unison, throwing dirt and rocks throughout the cave. Their bullets miss the outlaws. Panic-stricken, I freeze. I should pull the gun from my pocket and nail The Viper, even if I have to shoot him in the back. Is the gun in my pocket even loaded?

Time stands still, and thoughts bounce around my head as fast as bullets in the cave. What if I get shot? My fatherless children will be motherless also. How can I take such a chance? But then, what if I don't act? If Rose could shoot Bartholomieux, couldn't I shoot a monster like The Viper? I am accurate with firearms and I am a proven hunter. Could I shoot a man? I remind myself that The Viper is a murderer. There's no telling how many people he's killed.

I look toward the entrance and see Agapito. My heart drops.

Near me, a gun fires, and Agapito drops to the ground. I turn and look at The Radish, across from the small firepit. His gun still points toward the cave's entrance. The earth feels like it has given way beneath me, and my heart feels like it will implode within my chest.

Just inside the entrance, to the left of where Agapito stood, Landon Young lifts his revolver, points it at me, and I shudder when I see the blast from the barrel of his gun. I glance to my side in time to see Leon Humphries, or rather, Leon McAdams, fall to the ground with his head twisted grotesquely and a bullet hole just beneath his left ear.

That leaves The Radish, The Viper, and Sloan, who was injured yesterday. My heart pounds in my chest, and still, I fail to act. Agapito has been shot. I know that Landon Young is in the cave, but who else is here? How many men dove in? Perhaps a third man? What chance do two men who are unfamiliar with the interior of the cave stand against the three brothers who know their surroundings?

I look at Rose. Like an inchworm doubling back on itself, she slides her bottom along the cave floor, away from the fire and toward the dark perimeter. As if following Rose, Garland rolls like a log down a hill into the darkness. Barely visible in the darkness, somebody crouches near the rocky wall of the cave. When he blinks, I realize that it is Andrew. Good Heavens. What is he doing here? How could the men allow a boy his age to be a part of any rescue attempt?

Looking back at the rope, and gripping the gun in my pocket, I wonder. Did Andrew sneak into the cave in the middle of the night? How did he make it past the watchful outlaws? Why didn't he wake me?

Who ever heard of a woman battling gunslingers? I imagine Boss Wheel in my head, telling me to leave it to the men. My eyes pinch closed. What if, while trying to help the rescuers, I make matters worse? What if I miss and my bullet accidentally hits a friend instead of a foe? Should I do this? Once I start, I can't stop.

A voice appears in my ear—not in my thoughts, or in my head, but an actual voice. I turn my head slightly and look from the corner of my eye. There's nobody there. It sounded just like Boss Wheel. His dead body is still on the ground, but I heard him say, "She'll do."

What if the outlaws shoot me? My children will be left alone in this world, orphans. What choice do I have? The Viper plans to kill every man, woman, and child. Perhaps he'll spare Rose in hopes that she'll lead him to the money stolen by The Viper's father in Sullivan, Missouri. There's no chance that The Viper will honor her threats and let the rest of us live.

I look back at the entrance and see Agapito's crumpled body on the ground. There isn't time to think. Anger overwhelms me. It's time for action. I kick the loosened coils from my ankles, jump to my feet, and pull the gun from my pocket.

The brothers are focused on the attackers at the mouth of the cave. They don't know that my hands are free or that I'm armed.

Something must have caught The Viper's attention. His head turns slightly in my direction. Deliberately, I lift the gun and say a rare prayer in my head. The Viper is faster than I am. I shift to the left and cock my gun. A bullet skims my right arm and I swallow hard. It's all happening so fast, yet I'm aware of each fragment of a second.

I've been hit. The look on The Viper's face conveys disbelief. How could an expert outlaw miss at such close range? While he tries to figure out what went wrong, I squeeze the trigger. I did it. I shot the murderer. Can it be? Is he really dead? But I can't stop now. There are still two brothers remaining. We are still in danger.

Reminding myself that I can't stop until it's over, I spin to the right, grab my lasso, and throw my loop over The Radish as his gun blasts wildly. If only I could make sure the stray bullet didn't hit one of the children. I yank hard, wishing I were sitting in the saddle so Blizzard could pull The Radish through the fire's embers.

As I turn to look for Sloan, he discharges his weapon, and half a second later, another shooter's bullet tears into Sloan's chest. I glance to the right and see Alvah Nye lowering his gun. Sloan's hands reach to cover his wound as he collapses into the dirt and eternal slumber.

I pull my rope hard, dragging The Radish closer, and look by my feet at The Viper, whose piercing blue eyes gaze beams of hatred in my direction. His body isn't moving, but the force of his eyes upon me feels like he's beating his fists against me. I feel sick and terrified, but I lift my chin and sneer at him. "You're dying." I've never thought such things before, but I can't control myself. "I killed you, and I'm not sorry."

The Viper speaks his final words. Somehow, he manages to speak clearly, though his strength is quickly fading. "I could have been the most famous outlaw the world has ever known. My brothers should have lived like kings in a castle, overlooking the Pacific Ocean. They would never have wanted for anything. We could have stayed together forever." The Viper whimpers at me as his energy wanes. "A woman. I've been killed by a woman. It's shameful. So, that's it then? What was my life for? Just shameful."

A long, deathly silence descends upon us. The only movement comes from flickering flames as firelight casts shadows onto the rocky walls of the mine.

The Viper's scowl wilts into befuddlement. "How can it be?" Whatever he meant to say next is lost in a gurgle as death claims the would-be notorious outlaw.

The Radish makes another attempt to rise and I pull the rope again. Someone has untied Rose. Oblivious to danger, she approaches the youngest outlaw, squats before him, and plucks a thick rattlesnake from the ground like she's gathering firewood. The serpent shakes his rattles as Rose drops the creature into the fire. The dying snake squirms within the embers and gyrates. Its body cooks at the same time as its death throes move it about. Rose pulls a large handful of dried sage from her pocket, tosses it on the fire, and a large cloud of gray smoke envelopes her.

The lecherous boy dives forward, and I pull the rope again, foiling his attempt to tackle Rose. Alvah rushes in and subjugates The Radish.

I throw the rest of the wood on top of the snake, still twisting in the fire. The cave fills with light.

Just beyond the toe of my boots, something on the ground catches my eye. I bend over and pick up the shed skin of a snake. Is this the very skin of the snake that slithered along my body this morning? My thoughts travel back in time. It was just after we buried Ellen, Carter, and Larkin as we prepared to leave the Little Blue River when I found the ghostly remains of a giant snake's transformation. From early May to mid-September, so much has happened. So many things have changed, but I can't think about that.

Sadness quickly replaces my anger and fear as I stagger toward the exit. Tears wet my cheeks. Grief overwhelms me as I straighten Agapito's arms and legs into a more dignified burial position. What if I had acted more quickly? What if I had been braver? Could I have saved him?

I used to think I was unlucky in love, but now I am sure. It must be a full-fledged curse. Yet, in my mind, I hear his voice asking the question from long ago, "Does true love transcend time?"

My hands shake as I look at the hole in his shirt. It wasn't The Viper who shot him, yet it is The Viper's fault. But my cowardice is also to blame. My head droops and I begin to look away. I should go to my children now. Then, Agapito's lips move, his voice barely audible. "You have come for me, *estimada. Querida.*"

Dropping to my knees, I beg, "Do not die." My voice cracks. "Please stay with me." I lean forward, gently kiss his lips and remember the moment we shared so long ago at Scotts Bluff. It seems like a lifetime since then. "Stay with me, Agapito."

I turn toward the darkness behind me and shout at whoever is listening. "Get Dr. Appleyard. We must save Agapito. Please!"

Agapito gasps, and I fear that he has expired. I look back at him, and his face is tense with worry. Softly, he says, "Your arm, *querida*. You have been hit."

I look down and I am surprised to see blood. I have been shot. I hold my arm close to my side and blurt, "It's just a scratch. It really is nothing." I move my arm so that it is behind my back. "I can barely feel it. It is you we need to take care of."

Wearily, Agapito says, "Slow down, *querida*. I can not listen that fast." Then he fades into unconsciousness.

I'm sure that Agapito will die if we don't do something right away. I turn and scream, "Help! Please hurry."

Alvah limps past me, stopping for a moment to place his hand on my shoulder. "It looks like a bullet grazed my leg. Wayne Horton and Bobby Bond are also hurt. I'll ride for help."

I say, "Maybe I should go."

"No. Let *me* go, Dorcas. You stay with Agapito. I hog-tied The Sprout and left him beside the fire."

A voice from inside the mine shouts, "It's The Radish, not The Sprout."

Andrew, Garland, and Rose walk past me and sit in the sunlight just outside the mine. Rose turns toward me and says, "There are many tortured spirits in there, Mama."

I step toward her, stretch my injured arm, and grasp her shin. What do you say in response to such a statement? Nothing comes to mind.

She says, "They killed that miner, Mama. His bones lie under Agapito. The brothers laughed at him as they buried him beneath the entrance of the mine he discovered."

To think, she sees it as her responsibility to help tortured souls. Of all things! To Andrew, I say, "Where did you come from?"

"I had to come, Mama. I was so scared. I started to untie your hands, but the evil-eyed outlaw started to stir. I backed away into the darkness. I froze, Mama."

I can't convince him that he is a hero. It pains me to see him trembling. If he were younger and we were alone, I might wrap my arms around him. Instead, I lean forward and grasp his arm. "Oh, Andrew. I don't know what I would have done without your help." If it weren't for the gun he brought and his work on the knots at my wrist, there's no telling who might have been killed.

It's late afternoon when Alvah returns with helpers and a wagon. Dr. Appleyard examines Agapito, and then Alvah's posse carries the injured man on a hastily constructed stretcher to the rig.

Dr. Appleyard looks concerned and grumbles, "He's barely hanging on. I don't know if we can save him, Dorcas." When the assistant wagon master is safely aboard, the doctor drives the wagon slowly toward Farewell Bend, while Andrew, Garland and the other emigrants ride crowded inside. Alvah and I follow on horseback, and Rose sits behind me on Blizzard. The Radish sits on Clipper, Boss Wheel's horse, with his hands tied to the saddle horn. After crossing the Snake River, The Radish says, "Can you take me to our cabin? We should free the stock."

Alvah asks, "What stock? What cabin?"

The last outlaw tells the hunter about The Viper's compound. "It's just a couple of miles west, up Birch Creek to Chicken Creek."

Alvah looks at me and shakes his head. If I could read his mind, I might hear him saying to himself something like, "Why am I not surprised?"

When we reach The Viper's compound, Rose dismounts and walks across the rivulet. I look at Alvah and shrug. We follow her as Chicken Creek descends into a small oasis with a tiny pool of water and a small thicket of trees. A village of abandoned wagons appears before us. One wagon has a painted bonnet with faded lettering that reads, "Oregon or Bust" and "The Terwilligers." The outlaws killed Sarah's husband. She and her children fled to safety, but the outlaws made off with their wagon.

Alvah, The Radish, and I watch from the shade as Rose climbs aboard, one after the other. At one wagon, she puts her hands together in prayer in front of her face. In front of another wagon, she kneels and stretches her arms into the grass in front of her. Elsewhere, she lifts her arms toward the sky. When she returns to our side, her eyes are bloodshot, and her skin is ash gray. In her hands, she holds the gifts that Snarling Wolf gave her. I thought those had been left behind at Snarling Wolf's pyre. I mutter, "What in the Heavens are they doing here?"

The Radish tells us that his brother took them from an Indian's grave.

We walk back to the cabin and follow The Radish inside. He looks about as if remembering awful things that happened there. I ask, "Is there anything you'd like to bring with you?"

"What do you mean?"

"You can't stay here. You're coming with us."

"I thought you were going to hang me. Am I a prisoner?"

"I don't know. Maybe it is up to the wagon master or the captain. Perhaps it is up to you."

He walks over and picks up objects that must have belonged to his brothers. I say, "Your brothers loved you in their own way. It's not your fault that you never learned right from wrong. Yes, you were raised by scoundrels, but you can rise above your upbringing. The first thing you will need to understand is that you must respect women. Never force yourself upon us. Keep your hands to yourself until you can *win* a woman's heart. Understand?"

The Radish touches his belt buckle. He says, "Yes, ma'am," and quickly unhands the fastener. The holster is empty anyhow. His gun was left behind in the cave.

Alvah raises an unconvinced eyebrow at me. I'm sure he doubts whether there's any goodness to find within the teenaged scoundrel. With a frown, Alvah says, "Let's drive the stock back to Farewell Bend."

It seems like a miracle. I never thought we'd see Cobb's Devons again. As Alvah and The Radish drive oxen, donkeys, mules, and horses from the outlaws' grassy meadow, I'm inspired by the movement and gathering of the herd. Wouldn't it be something to have a ranch instead of a farm? When I spy the black Appaloosa, I clap, giddy with joy. What a relief to find Dembi Koofai's horse. Then, I see my beloved mustang among the herd of rescued stock, tossing her head and throwing her mane about. Beside Gwibunzi runs a familiar looking cremello. "Oh, Alvah. That's Larry Pritchard's brother's horse, Señorita."

In my head, I hear the question, "What's your dream? Not Larkin's dream, but yours?" I wish I knew. One thing's for certain. The sight of my wild mustang fills me with joy.

Wild horses can be tamed, and people can too. Boss Wheel changed. Couldn't The Radish change too?

At camp, a crowd gathers as we ride in with The Radish. Christopher asks him, "Are you an outlaw?"

The Radish frowns, looks at me, and answers, "I used to be."

I tell the young man that he can toss his things under our wagon.

Captain Meadows looks at me, his head pitched forward and brow furrowed. "You can't keep that murderer. *He* is not some kind of pet. He needs to be tried, convicted, and hung."

Instead of addressing the man as Captain, I say, "Reverend Meadows, he's merely a boy. We buried the murderous outlaws. We must save this child. I'm sure that Jesus would want us to show him mercy, and teach him love and kindness."

The middle-aged preacher squirms while considering my words. After a long, reflective moment, he says, "I will meet with the boy, alone, and determine whether he is repentant. Then, I will decide whether we shall have a trial or a prayer service."

I nod, gratefully. Under the circumstances, I can't ask for more. I say, "Thank you, Reverend." As the crowd dissipates, I introduce The Radish to Stillman and the children. Then, I speak to the former gunslinger. "May we call you by your given name instead?"

The boy shakes like a dog climbing from a river and says, "Sure. My name is Ross."

Christopher laughs. "Ross, The Radish."

He closes his eyes and speaks with them shut. "No, just Ross. I'm done with *The Radish*."

I pat the young man on his shoulder and make my way to the wagon master's camp. Careful not to rock the wagon, I tiptoe aboard and look at Agapito's angelic expression. He is shirtless. Bandages wind around his chest and over his shoulder. I've never seen him when he wasn't fully dressed, and I can't help but gaze with a bit of longing in my heart. If only he weren't injured. I don't want to wake him, but I fear that he will catch a chill. I lift a thick blanket from a box beside the bed board and drape it over him.

His lips move, and he swallows, but other than that, he is like a corpse in a casket.

We bury our dead as the sun sets. Reverend Meadows says Heavenly words over the graves of Clarkson Sawyer, who was killed in the first volley, and Hannah Knox. Then, the scouts shovel dirt over their dead bodies.

When he finishes his prayers, the man says, "I'm sorry to conduct official business so soon after a burial and on a Sunday. But we have three important matters to address. They can't wait." First, Captain Meadows asks whether anyone objects to Wade and Dottie Crouse's offer to adopt Teddy Sawyer. When he asks, he looks directly at the boy's grandfather, the loner from New Jersey, Sully Pierce.

The man nods assent and says, "Provided the Crouse family doesn't mind me living nearby and visiting the boy whenever I want to." I think back to when the child's mother's dress caught fire. Poor Bridget Sawyer was the first casualty of our forsaken journey, and now, Teddy's father is gone too.

Then, the self-appointed mayor of our rolling village addresses the matter of our prisoner. "I have met with the young fella, Ross McAdams. He is a sinner, plain and simple. He doesn't deny it. His is a sad and tortured story, abused by his parents first, and then his brothers after that." The man looks directly at me and says, "At first, I would have argued for justice. After talking with the boy, I think we should show him mercy. Mrs. Moon has offered to let the boy travel with her family to Oregon. Does anyone object?"

The travelers look at each other as if wondering whether anybody will voice a concern.

Galusha Gains shouts, "I want to see him hang."

Samuel Grosvenor rubs his hands together and has an excited look on his face. "Me too."

Oona Reid observes, "I knew something terrible was going to happen."

Horace Blocker says, "We could have all been killed. We'll probably all die anyway. We'll never make it to Oregon."

Esther Bump rocks Plumjohn in the crook of her arm. She says, "Think of all the people who were robbed or murdered. Don't they deserve justice? That scoundrel needs to pay for what him and his brothers done."

Landon Young agrees. "Last year, the gang killed my sister's husband. Now, their children must grow up without a father. Think of them. How many other people died at the hands of these butchers?"

Nobody wants to speak for Ross McAdams. I step forward and take a deep breath. I hope the words come to me. I remind them of what Captain Meadows said and add the details I know about Ross' tragic childhood.

Galusha and Samuel grumble objections while I speak, but the crowd is otherwise silent. When I'm done, Captain Meadows asks if anyone else would like to say anything.

Ross takes off his hat and holds it over his chest. He looks from one person to another and slowly says, "I'm real sorry. I reckon it don't count for much to say I didn't know any better. It's like Mrs. Moon said. Nobody taught me right from wrong, but I learn fast. Gimme a chance. You won't regret it. I promise."

The tittering crowd makes a variety of noises. People whisper into their neighbors' ears, and the crowd mulls about. Captain Meadows watches and listens patiently. Then, after a couple of minutes, he clears his throat and raises his hand. Quiet spreads across the travel-weary crowd. Captain Meadows says, "I recommend a conditional forgiveness. Give the boy a week to prove himself. We'll vote next week. If you still want to hang him, we'll string him up then."

A handful of people disagree, but the majority votes in favor of Captain Meadow's suggestion. The crowd begins to wander away. The Captain raises his voice. "Attention, travelers. We have another matter to consider. With the death of Joseph Roulette and the incapacity of the assistant wagon master, we need to hire a new wagon master. I propose we employ Alvah Nye. Anyone else have a suggestion?"

The hunter, Galusha Gains, says that Alvah is too young, and his sidekick agrees. "What about Wade Crouse or Travis Latham? They're at least in their thirties. How about the surveyor? What's his name again? Or maybe one of hunters? I suppose I could do the job."

The map maker, Fritz Franzwa, scratches his clean shaven cheek. He shakes his head, and the bearded half of his face sways with the movement of his head. He says, "I'll do anything I can to help, but I don't want the job of wagon master. Young Mr. Nye is perfectly suited to lead us, with the help of our scouts." Mr. Franzwa gestures with his extended arm toward Alvah Nye, who stands between Arikta and Dembi Koofai. "It would appear that the scouts have decided who they'd like to lead us."

Committeeman Travis Latham stands forward and tells the crowd that he appreciates the mention, but he's not the man for the job. "I'm not good with a gun."

The third member of The Committee, Wade Crouse, steps forward holding his newly adopted young son in his arms. He says he'd take the job if there weren't any other options. "I'm better at surviving in a town than in the wilderness." Then, Mr. Crouse throws his support behind Alvah Nye.

The new boss steps forward, having won the job without speaking a word on his own behalf. He tips his hat and says, "Appreciate the confidence. I'll do my level best to see to your safety and keep everyone fed. We still got a long way to travel. But I accept the job of *assistant* wagon master only. When Agapito recovers, he can take the top job."

Does Alvah really believe that Agapito will recover? Is there hope?

Arikta hands Alvah the trumpet. The new assistant wagon master takes a deep breath and puts the instrument to his lips. After several pitiful blows, Alvah hands it back to Arikta. "You'd better tend to Reveille, friend."

The Pawnee scout blows three strong notes on the bugle, demonstrating that he has the ability to wake us in the morning, even if he can't play a tune.

After dark, Rose and I climb the hillside overlooking Farewell Bend, accompanied by Arikta and Dembi Koofai. Earlier in the day, we buried Joseph Roulette on the prominence. It's a splendid vantage point and most appropriate for the former mountain man to watch over the migratory trail, in perpetuity. The gruff guide can watch over loco greenhorns as they begin their final push toward the western coast.

We should return to camp, but a brilliant sunset holds us until the colors fade to gray.

Monday, September 16

So much has happened, and so many things have changed, it hardly feels like the same expedition. When the wagons begin to move, I climb up into the back of the wagon master's rig.

I've barely left Agapito's side since returning to camp after liberating stolen stock from the outlaws' enclave. Hollis and Charlotte check on our patient frequently, but his condition has not improved. Sometimes, I think that he's awake, but he doesn't open his eyes. He grumbles and attempts to move, perhaps intending to roll onto his side, but he is unable to turn, remaining instead on his back. When sweat appears on his brow, I remove the blanket that covers him. And then, when he shivers, I replace the quilt to keep him comfortable.

A short distance up the trail, Arikta pops his head into the back of the wagon. "Get ready for a rough ride. This stretch is steep and bumpy." I'm disinclined to heed the scout's warning, as it seems that so much of our journey could be similarly described. Before long, Agapito is jostled this way and that, and I do my best to keep him from rolling off the planks that serve as a bed in the back of the wagon. Then, the wagon begins to tip upward, and Agapito slides toward the back of the wagon. I pin him with my wrists, under his arms, desperately trying to avoid bumping his wound, and wonder whether I'll be able to keep him safely in place.

When we finally reach a more level stretch of trail, I tie Agapito down as if he were freight. It doesn't seem right, but I worry that I will tire and be unable to hold him in place. Hoping it will make him more comfortable, I cushion the rough rope with all the fabric garments I can find. When the wagon wheels roll across the roughest, rockiest section of trail, Agapito's head is tossed away from me, but his body remains safely in place.

Later, as the day warms, Agapito's brow remains sweaty even when the blanket is removed. With moist washcloths, I dab his forehead, and he begins to moan. Finally, after several hours, his eyes flutter open and he says, "*Dios mío, querida*. Am I a prisoner?"

"Heavens, no." I realize that I've shouted at him when his eyes stretch open widely, wider than I've ever seen before.

"Oh, Agapito. I'm sorry. I have startled you. I couldn't help myself. You've come back to us. We were so worried."

His eyebrows flicker as I prattle on, then, when I'm quiet, he gently nods his head, looking into my eyes for confirmation. "I have been shot."

"Yes."

He looks at the small bandage on my arm. "But you are safe?" His head turns to see if we are alone. "And Rose?"

"Yes, she is safe as well."

Agapito's brow furrows and it looks like he's searching his memory for what he can recall about the outlaws and the cave. I take his hand in my hands and wish that I had better news for him. He asks, "What has happened?"

I lean forward, straighten a ruffled clump of hair beside his ear, and begin to tell him the story. Evidently, he was aware of and recalled the deaths of Clarkson Sawyer and Hannah Knox. When I get to the part where The Viper shot and killed Boss Wheel, Agapito gasps. "Oh no, *querida*. It can not be." He blinks hard, as if it pains him to ask another question, then blurts several in a row. "What day is it now? Where are we? Is everybody else alright? Who is wagon master now?"

"It's Monday. We left the Snake River this morning. Bobby, Wayne, and Alvah have minor injuries, but everybody else is fine. You are wagon master, and we voted Alvah Nye assistant wagon master. He's in charge until you've healed."

His lower lip quivers. "Oh, Dorcas. I know I told you we were almost there. The truth is, the road ahead is hard. There are many challenges ahead, and we must hurry. Winter is coming." His eyes look down along his cheeks and he struggles to lift his head so he can see his body. "How bad am I hurt?"

"We're not sure. The bullet hit your left shoulder, almost your chest. Hollis thinks you are lucky it didn't hit your heart or lungs, but it came very close."

The corner of Agapito's mouth turns up slightly, and he jokes, "Lucky? Luckier if a bullet did not hit me at all, *querida*."

The patient quickly tires and I urge him to take a drink before he rests. It's hard to pour water into a man's mouth when he's on his back, but I manage to help him tip his head forward, my hand behind his head. When he's done, I wipe the corners of his mouth.

"*Gracias. Tan cansado.*" I guess his words mean that he is tired. He closes his eyes, and his head rolls to the side.

It is such a relief to see Agapito return to consciousness, but worrisome to see him so weak. The bullet may have missed his vital organs, but his injury has sapped his strength. Hollis isn't worried about paralysis. Agapito can't seem to command his body beyond moving his head, though I must remember that he is tied to a board.

When the wagons stop, Arikta says we've only traveled about ten miles. Stillman takes my place beside Agapito while I step off for a break. When I return, Stillman whispers, "The bullet that killed Hannah Knox was meant for me. It might sound crazy, but I heard Carter's voice whisper in my ear. I even felt the breeze of his breath and it gives me gooseflesh just thinking of it. He said, 'Duck,' just as The Viper pulled the trigger. I swear, I heard him and did what he said. When I dropped to the ground, Miss Knox was shot. That poor woman would still be alive if it weren't for me."

"Oh, Stillman. You mustn't blame yourself. You were not meant to catch a bullet." I pull the young man close and stroke the back of his head. "It is the Viper who is to blame. Not you."

When Stillman is gone and I'm alone with Agapito again, I mumble to myself, "Now, even Stillman thinks he's hearing ghosts. What next?" Then, I remember thinking I heard Boss Wheel whisper into my ear before I shot The Viper.

Agapito doesn't regain consciousness again, and sleeps through the afternoon and evening. I take another break as the sun begins to set. I don't know the name of the waterway nearby, but the brilliant orange and salmon hues from the setting sun reflect brilliantly on the placid water's surface. I should be glad that our journey is approaching its conclusion, but will I miss the adventure?

If only Agapito's life weren't in jeopardy.

Tuesday, September 17

A scene unfolds before my eyes on my way back from my morning trip to the ladies' latrine. Ross stands, holding an empty bucket on his way to fetch water from the creek. His mouth hangs open and his shoulders hunch forward. His gaze is fixed on a woman dipping her pail into the water. I'm all too familiar with Ross's interest in the fairer sex. It should be no surprise that Berta Lett has caught his eye.

When the young woman stands and turns, she sees the lanky outlaw and drops her bucket. She stares at him, evidently oblivious to the water that soaks her bare feet. The expression on her face is not one of fear or shock. Have I just witnessed that instant when young lovers realize their destiny, in an instant—love at first sight?

Miranda Knox appears beside me, having finished answering the call of nature, herself. With disgust, she proclaims, "I declare, what have we here? That criminal is ogling this poor young woman. Do something, before he ravages her."

Berta's brother, Carl, arrives, breathless. To his sister, he says, "What's keeping you?"

The young woman mutters something about "shpillink da vater."

Ross finally finds his ability to speak and steps toward Berta and her bucket. "Allow me."

Miranda stomps her foot. "Why must we harbor this fugitive? His brother killed my sister, and there's no telling how many people this Devil's spawn has murdered himself."

Ross turns toward Miranda and says, "I'm sorry about your sister, ma'am. But I don't think I've killed anybody. My job was stealing horses and rustling cattle, I'm not proud to say."

"But you did shoot the Mexican. Everybody's talking about it."

Ross hangs his head. "It's true. I think I did shoot *him*. We were under attack. I had to do it." Ross pauses for a moment, and then continues. "If he dies, then I *did* kill a man." Then Ross looks at me.

In the confusion of the moment, I hadn't realized that it was Ross who shot Agapito. Does this change how I feel about the boy? He couldn't avoid being an outlaw any more than Gwibunzi could help being a wild mustang. And, if Ross hadn't fired at Agapito, one of his brothers would have, I suppose. Having already decided to reform The Radish, I stubbornly insist that he could not help it. He just needs a chance to follow the straight and narrow path. Yet, this talk about Agapito's possible death troubles me.

Miranda expresses exasperation with a judgmental sigh and marches off in a huff. Previously, I had always thought of her as kind and gentle, but some people don't believe in second chances. It is as if Hannah's gruffness were left behind when she passed away, and picked up by her sister.

Berta follows her brother back to camp, looking back over her shoulder at Ross.

When Berta finally disappears around the back corner of a wagon, Ross's lanky frame sags. He turns, looks at me with lost puppy eyes, and says, "Who was *that*?!"

"The young German woman?" What a silly question. He certainly isn't curious about Miranda or Carl.

He nods, slowly, as if still mesmerized.

"That's Berta Lett. I take it you're smitten?"

"If I had a girl like that, I'd marry her in an instant. I'd never want another woman. I swear."

So much for the wayward outlaw who dreamed of bedding hundreds of women.

After a grueling, twelve mile-trek, mostly uphill, we reach Durkee Creek and settle in for the evening. Agapito was awake for a couple of hours in the morning, and a half an hour in the afternoon. Mostly, he was groggy, and slurred Spanish words that I couldn't understand.

When supper is finished, Ross climbs into the wagon master's rig and sits beside me, silent for a few minutes as I comb Agapito's hair.

Ross asks, "Is that a mane comb?"

"It is. I bought it from Muddy George, the peddler." I look at Ross as I think about the kindly traveling merchant. "We found him dead at Alkali Springs." It's hard to forget the grisly scene we encountered just four days ago. Recalling his brutal murder makes me question my sanity. Surely, Ross's parents and brothers are to blame, but it's hard to overlook whatever role Ross must have played.

Ross's back hunches, his head hangs, and he speaks into his lap. "I should a never listened to The Viper. I could a run away a hundred times, but instead, I just did what he told me. I figger I knew better, but didn't let myself think a running off much. Never could get over listening to people scream when they died. Couldn't watch when they begged for their lives. Used to try and stop The Viper from killing 'em, but when I did, he turned meaner. It's like he became somebody else. Strange thing is, he loved us, Leon, Sloan, and me, in his own way. I swear he did."

Whenever Ross talks about his upbringing, to me, it makes me sick and sad at the same time. I can't help feeling sorry for the youngest brother that never knew any better, even though he says, deep down, that he did. Yet, Ross was almost like a prisoner within his own family. With the parents he had, and his siblings, how could he have broken free on his own?

I'm startled to hear Agapito speak, and realize that I have been stroking his arm while talking to Ross.

"*Me duele mucho la barriga.*"

"I am sorry, Agapito. I don't understand."

"*Lo siento, querida*. My belly hurts. I have the hunger and the thirst."

I help Agapito drink from a canteen as I promise to get him something to eat.

He sees that we are not alone, raises an eyebrow at the sight of a stranger, and says, "This is the one that shot me, no?"

"Oh, Agapito. This is Ross. Ross McAdams. You must try to forgive him."

"It will be hard, *querida*. I will think about it. If you say I should forgive him, there must be a reason. But it is a lot to forgive." Agapito looks at me with a pitiful expression and says, "I would do anything for a lemon scone, Dead Aim Dorcas."

Wednesday, September 18

Folks mull about The Hub after we settle into a nice campground beside the Powder River. The sound of raised voices draws me from the wagon master's rig, and I step toward the center of the ring.

On my way, I look to the north and see the snow-capped Blue Mountains. Their breathtaking beauty provides a feast for the eyes, and yet, the jagged white tips are a harsh reminder that we are behind schedule. If we had not taken Sundays off, as the good Lord and Captain Meadows ordain, we might already have reached our destination.

After a twenty-three mile day, everyone should be exhausted. Instead, they seem riled, like a frenzied mob. The same travelers who silently plodded along during the heat of summer now gripe endlessly. Though we have left the Snake River, which Boss Wheel blamed for turning greenhorns loco, we seem no closer to rekindling our sensibilities. Our rolling village has endured a lot. It's hard not to think of tragedy, especially after our ordeal at Farewell Bend. I understand how people feel after months in the wilderness. Our trip has been plagued by the loss of so many loved ones. Our friends and family members are gone forever. Though they knew the perilous journey exposed us to many dangers, we made the decision to take these risks for the sake of opportunity, new beginnings, and adventure. I buried my husband beside the Little Blue River, and now, I dread the next disaster. What if the next casualty of the trail is Agapito? Are his injuries life-threatening? Just the thought of his death horrifies me, and I struggle to force the notion from my mind.

With a deep breath, I halt and stand among the crowd. I glance about to see whose voices rise above the din. Galusha Gains says, "We should have taken the cutoff. Maybe then, Clarkson Sawyer, Hannah Knox, and Boss Wheel would still be alive."

Arikta says, "Probably most of you would be dead and buried."

Miranda rants, "As if we haven't had enough to overcome, now we must face snow." She spits the last word from her lips with a sneer.

Bobby looks around, accusingly. "Who says?"

Wayne answers, "It's in the paper. Read it for yourself."

Bobby says, "Save me the trouble."

Miranda lifts the lid that protects *The Rolling Home Times* from the elements. She taps the paper for emphasis. "It says so right here. Colder tonight. First snow within a week."

Galusha Gains, who probably still thinks Rose is a witch, says, "It's bad enough that child-wizard conjured up bloodthirsty outlaws and a torrid heat spell. Now he's bringing snowstorms down upon us."

Andrew says, "I'm not a wizard. I don't conjure things. It's just, sometimes, I can tell what's going to happen before it does. Mostly, it's just the weather.

It's not my fault. It pops into my head, I write it down, and then it turns out to be true. Maybe I'm just a good guesser."

Samuel Grosvenor belches, and adds a harrumph.

Galusha prods Andrew, "Why don't you conjure up a feast. I'm tired of eating the same dang vittles every stinking day."

The urge to come to my son's defense is strong, but I resist. Though I once bristled when Larkin told me not to coddle them, five months on the trail have matured the boys to the point where they no longer welcome motherly interventions. It's hard to believe they aren't older than they are.

Samuel says, "Nevermind the kid. When do we string up the outlaw?"

Galusha adds, "I don't know what we're waiting for. A knife in the back? A whack on the back of the head? A bullet in the gizzard? We've seen what his kind is capable of."

As he often does, Horace says, "What difference does it make? We're all going to die anyway."

Samuel cusses. "You, maybe, but I don't plan on it. I have no intention of leaving my bones along this forsaken trail."

Galusha says, "What about our womenfolk? I've seen the way that Radish gawks at the women, especially that little German girl."

Bobby says, "He's been fawning all over her. Follows her everywhere she goes, ever since yesterday. Fetches her water, builds her fire, does all her chores. I bet he's just waiting for a chance to have his way with her."

I've held my tongue long enough. "So the young man, Ross, has been nice to Berta and her family. For that, you want to condemn him? We're supposed to be giving him a chance to show he's repentant. I think he *has* changed. Wouldn't you say helping people should be commended? As for making eyes at Berta, Ross is single, but I've seen many of you *married* fellows leering at that pretty young thing instead of minding your own manners."

Bobby says, "What about justice? Him and his brothers are criminals. I want to see him swing."

A voice from behind me causes me to turn. Landon Young says, "Don't forget my sister's husband, killed by these pirates last year. Do it for Sarah. Sarah Terwilliger. She craves vengeance. She deserves to know that justice has been served. When we reach Oregon City, I want to tell her that those men that killed her husband are dead."

I thought more people would want to give Ross a chance to repent and reform. But there are many who prefer to take his life to make up for the innocent people his brothers killed. No matter how hard I try to see their side of the matter, I can't agree. Would I feel differently if Agapito were to die from his wounds?

Alvah strides through the crowd, tells Wayne and Bobby they have first watch, and assigns Galusha and Samuel to the second shift. As he walks away, all four men grumble, and Galusha laments, "We should never have elected that one to be in charge." I can't comprehend the basis of Galusha's objection. We all take our turns on night watch. Galusha spits beside my feet when I offer to take his turn, which I interpret to be a rejection of my offer.

A childish interruption provides a welcome break. Dahlia Jane runs toward the river, shouting, "Mama, look. It's a cat." Her little legs carry her faster than I've ever seen her run before. "Here, kitty, kitty."

Galusha says, "Stupid child. That's a polecat, not a kitten. What would a house cat be doing here?"

Arikta says, "You would be surprised. Sometimes people bring them. We discourage it. Boss Wheel said he only seen one cat make it from Independence to Oregon City."

The skunk easily outruns the child, but instead of disappearing into the wilderness, the critter doubles back, zigzags through the gathered crowd, lifts its tail, and sprays me. It's over in a moment, but I'm drenched in its rotten musk.

Thursday, September 19

IN THE MORNING, AGAPITO awakens with a snort. *"¿Qué apesta? Dios mío. ¿Es la muerte?* No, not in Spanish. In English. What stinks? Is it me? Did I die?"

"Good Heavens, Agapito. No. You had better not go and die. Dahlia Jane chased after a cat, only it was a skunk. The wretched creature perfumed me generously."

Agapito crinkles his nose. *"No es bueno."* He closes his eyes, but a pained expression remains on his face. "Get the doctor for me, *por favor.*"

My stomach does a somersault. I want to ask Agapito why, but hurry off to get Hollis, assuming the need is urgent. As predicted, it was colder overnight, and my feet crunch through frozen blades of grass. I glance at the frost covered landscape, and summon the doctor. Fortunately, Hollis and Charlotte are awake in the next wagon. I might have hollered over, rather than stepping off to get him.

When Hollis climbs into the wagon, Agapito is still awake. He says, "I want you to remove that bullet, Doctor. It is still inside me, no?"

I thought that the bullet had been removed while we were at the outlaw's compound, and express alarm to learn otherwise.

Hollis says, "It could set your recovery back. I might not be able to get it out, and I could damage your wound more than it already is. You will have to start your recovery all over again."

Agapito says, "I do not care. I must forgive the man who shot me, but I can not do it if I must carry his bullet in my chest."

I say, "You can't operate while we travel, Hollis. Is it better to do it in the morning or the evening? How long does it take?"

Hollis answers. "I can't say. I won't know how difficult it is until I get started, and I don't have a lot of experience with such surgeries."

Agapito says, "I understand, Doctor. I will take my chances. Tonight it is."

Hollis tells Agapito to try and rest as much as he can during the day.

As I tie Agapito to the board, he says, "What choice do I have? I could not get up if I wanted to." He flashes a sweet but tired grin at me, and it gladdens me to see the dimple near the corner of his mouth.

I would like to remain beside Agapito during the surgery, but it isn't possible. Hollis says that a physician needs plenty of "elbow room, shoulder room, and doesn't like to be crowded." But he does need his assistant, and

Charlotte is an expert nurse. I ask myself what I can do, and remember Agapito's request for scones.

Since Agapito was shot, I haven't spent much time with my family. Since our wagon is next to the wagon master's, I'm able to keep an eye on them, even when I'm caring for Agapito. They've finished dinner and sit around a dwindling fire. It doesn't seem as if they are enjoying each other's company. Rose sits facing away from the fire, staring off into the distance. Stillman pokes purposelessly at the embers with a stick. Ross is stretched out on his back with his long legs crossed at his ankles, looking at the sky. Andrew and Christopher sit together, facing slightly away from one another, as if they've just given up on an argument. I prepare to ask where Dahlia Jane is, and then notice her at Cobb's camp, next door, playing with Bess and Joe as usual.

"Who wants to help me make scones?"

Andrew grumbles, rises to his feet, and gets the ingredients from the wagon. Christopher offers to build up the fire. Rose doesn't move, but Ross sits up and crosses his legs. I suggest, "How about some music? Could you play for us, Stillman?"

As I begin combining ingredients, Stillman fiddles with the Jew's harp, improving the family's mood. When he finishes a short song, Ross says, "I used to have one looked just like that. Don't know what happened to it. Always losing stuff. Can I try?"

Stillman frowns when Ross dutifully cleans the instrument as if dirt were caked onto it. Finally, Ross begins to play, and as I'm packing scone batter into the Dutch oven, I try to recall where we found the harp. "Good heavens, I just remembered." My outburst startles everyone, and Ross stops playing. "I think I have something that belongs to you, Ross. Maybe you'd like to have it back." I dig my hand into the pocket of my dress, but it isn't there. "It must be in my other dress pocket." I hurry off to get it, and scurry back with the bandana in hand.

Andrew says, "I thought I told you to get rid of that thing."

Ross's eyes light up when I hand him the neckerchief. "How did you come by this? I can't remember how long it's been missing."

I think back and describe the hillside where I found it tangled in the tortured branches of a miserable shrub.

Ross reflects. "We all had one. My sister made them, and sewed our names in them. That was just before The Viper shot her. But that was an accident." Ross crumples the bandana in his hand as if trying to hide it away.

Rose turns and says, "Olivia wants you to wear it. You need to remember how it was so you don't go back to being an outlaw. Every time you see or touch it, remember you have changed. She is proud of you. No more killing. No more thievery. Treat people nice. Understand?"

The former bandit nods in awe, and firelight illuminates his cheeks as Rose turns her head back away from us, slowly, as if watching somebody walking away.

As Ross ties the bandana around his neck, he says, "I declare. It felt just like Olivia was here, talking to me herself." He tightens the knot as if to be sure it will not come undone and be lost again. "It's a miracle. Makes my skin tingle. Spooky," he says, stretching out the word.

I don't know how Rose does it. Preposterous as it seems, I almost believe that Ross's sister, Olivia, whispered those words in her ear tonight. I guess I should also believe Carter saved Stillman's life.

The sun sets as the boys play song after song. I set a couple of scones aside for Agapito and step away from the fire. How long has it been? When will it be over? How long does it take a doctor to remove a bullet? I take a tentative step toward the back of the wagon master's rig, and Hollis emerges.

My hands clasp together beneath my chin, and I say Agapito's name.

Hollis says, "The slug was stuck in a bone, but I finally got it out."

"Is he alright?"

"He's breathing. Faintly."

"Will he live?"

"I can't say, Dorcas. I'm sorry. Pray for him."

My hand covers my mouth.

"Go to him."

I touch Hollis's shoulder briefly before dashing toward the wagon. My ears barely catch the doctor's advice. "Tell him you love him."

Friday, September 20

I remain beside Agapito all night. His breathing remains shallow, and I watch his chest as it expands and contracts. At one point, I worry that he has stopped breathing entirely. I recall Hollis's advice, lean forward, and whisper in Agapito's ear. "I love you, Agapito." He takes a shallow breath, and I tip my head back. I whisper through the wagon's bonnet. "Thank Heavens."

At Dawn, Charlotte sits beside me. "You haven't slept a wink, have you?"

"No. I'm worried."

"I know you are. It is out of our hands now. Beyond our control. Why don't you take a break. I'll sit with Agapito for a while."

I release my hold on the man's hand. "I know it sounds silly, but would you hold his hand while I'm gone? Somehow, I think it helps."

"Alright, dear."

The trumpet blasts as I step to the ground. Arikta stows the bugle. I update the scouts and plead for an easy day.

Dembi Koofai says, "Shor' day today."

Arikta says, "It's about twelve miles to Ladd Creek. The trail is rough, but we will go slow."

Dembi Koofai concurs. "Ver' rocky." I realize I must be frowning when he adds, "I am sorry." He pauses as if considering whether to add another word to his sentence, and then he repeats, "I am sorry, *estimada*." I'm touched by the scout's use of Agapito's endearing term.

"I shall have to secure Agapito to the bed plank again today."

Both scouts nod, and Arikta agrees, "It must be so."

I join my family for a cold, dry breakfast before preparing for the day's journey.

To Andrew, I say, "Sunny today?"

He shakes his head. "Bad weather is coming, Mama. Maybe today. Maybe tomorrow."

As Christopher and Stillman hitch up the oxen, Ross races off with a pail. I look at Andrew and he scoffs. "He's off to help the Germans. Maybe he should just move in with them."

Rose leads Dahlia Jane off to answer nature's call, and I ask Andrew to try and understand how Ross feels. "Young men Ross's age fall in love easily and can't think of anything else." A pang of worry twinges in my belly, and I must admit, if briefly, that love can be that way at any age. I should stay beside Agapito, but my family needs me too. "Someday, Andrew, you'll be just like Ross, obsessed and lovesick. You'll see." Maybe it is time to give up on the idea of being a woman alone. I can't help loving Agapito. It's the last thing I wanted, to love another man who won't love me back, but I can't help myself. I suppose it's just the way I am. I may as well accept it.

"Tell everyone to be careful today, Andrew. The scouts say the road ahead is rough."

When the wagons come to a stop, I peek out the back and then the front of the wagon. I realize that we have not circled up, but rather, we remain in a continuous line. With a glance to either side, I understand why. In the narrow gorge, there's barely enough room for the wagons, and the trickling creek beside the trail. I turn, look back at Agapito, and gasp. His antelope eyes are open and he's looking at me.

I hurry to his side, take his hand, and tell that him I am glad he is awake.

He whispers his words, barely formed. It must take great effort to speak. "Hollis get the bullet out?"

I nod.

"It is good. I am glad." He grimaces, and I wish there were a way to help him with the pain. Then he says, "Where are we?"

"Arikta and Dembi Koofai said that we would spend the night in Ladd Canyon. We just stopped. I think we are camped for the night, but we aren't circled up."

"Cannot circle in canyon." He turns his head, slightly to the left and then the right. "Cannot feel my legs. Why?"

"Maybe I tied you too tightly." I hasten to unwind the knots that have kept him in place despite the pitching movement of the wagon along the rocky trail. "Is that better?"

"Cannot feel my arms either, *querida*. Did the sawbones remove them?"

"Gracious sakes, no, Agapito."

He yawns. "I am tired. And, I am tired of being tired. If only..." His words trail away, his eyes close, and his head lolls to the right. My heart thunders in my chest. Is that it? Has he died?

I place one hand over his heart, and the other in front of his face. "Fight for me. Stay with me, Agapito. We need you. I need you." His breath is shallow, but he's alive. His chest expands slightly, and the air moves between his slightly parted lips. I add the words, "I love you," and feel anxious when I realize that I'm not alone. I look to the back of the wagon and see Stillman.

He climbs aboard and whispers, "I knew it. I just knew it. It's about time you realized it too. Now what?"

I shush him. "Good Heavens, Stillman. What are you doing, sneaking up on me like that?"

He ignores my question and sits beside me. After he inquires about Agapito's condition and I answer, he says, "Why should we pardon Ross? I'm all for second chances, but don't the victims deserve to have justice done?"

"Don't you like him?"

Stillman shrugs.

"You have to understand, he hasn't been around people much. He grew up alone on the frontier, just his parents and siblings. His mother beat them, his pa was a bank robber and a drunk, and his brothers followed the outlaw trail. What chance did he have to turn out differently?"

"I guess. But, still, think of all those victims. Imagine how frightened they were. And what about when they kidnapped Rose? Weren't you scared?"

"Plenty of people feel that way, Stillman. But what if Ross has the opportunity to make something of himself? What if he can help others who are headed down the wrong path find the right way instead? Wouldn't that be something?"

"Most say he'll go back to his old ways. How will we feel then, knowing we could have prevented it?"

"Has everyone decided?"

Stillman says, "I think so." He stands and says he has to get ready for night watch. "It's me and Horace Blocker tonight." He frowns and I don't envy him.

Saturday, September 21

In the morning, Agapito is breathing better, but he still feels disconnected from his limbs. He struggles to open his eyes and speak. When he finally comes to, his words don't make any sense. They don't sound like English, or Spanish either. Hollis warned me this might happen, but it is disconcerting, nevertheless. I speak to Agapito, hoping to reassure him, and gently stroke his arm so he'll know that he is not alone. What do people think when they're delirious? Do they believe they are forming words?

After a couple of minutes, Agapito falls back to sleep and I step from the wagon, rubbing my eyes. I must have slumbered, but I'm not sure how long. I'm surprised to see a dusting of snow on the ground, and gritty dry flakes spitting from the overcast sky. Andrew said the weather was going to take a turn for the worse.

We're told to expect a long bumpy ride, downhill. After that, we'll cross the Grande Ronde River, and spend Sunday on the other side. When Andrew shoves the post that houses *The Rolling Home Times* into the wagon master's prairie schooner, I'm curious. He's never done so before. Perhaps the others are in the way at the back of our wagon this morning.

Before we depart, Stillman brings Dahlia Jane and her dolly by. "She wants to ride with you today."

As the wheels begin to turn, the snow changes to rain, light at first, and then heavier. I feel sorry for my fellow travelers who will march alongside today. If it weren't for the need to succor Agapito, I would be challenging myself to trek along without complaint. Occasionally, a fat drop of water accumulates on the inside of the canvas wagon cover and then drops heavily onto us. Whenever that happens, I remind myself to be grateful for the protection it provides rather than complain about the occasional drop of water that permeates the bonnet.

After an hour of worsening weather, I peek through the small opening at the front of the wagon and notice that the small waterway we're following is spilling over its banks. Arikta rides by, shouting, "Keep 'em moving. Don't dally. We need to get through the gorge, fast. It might flood." I'm not sure who is driving the wagon master's team today, but I hear the whip crack and the wagon jostles on account of the extra speed.

When we emerge from Ladd Canyon, the wagons slow. It is reassuring to know that we're not traveling between mountains any longer.

Arikta passes by again with another warning. "Keep 'em moving. We have cleared Ladd Canyon, but we still must make it through Coyote Canyon before reaching the crossing at Grande Ronde." It's bad enough to have to worry about Agapito, flash floods, and another river crossing. Why must we traverse a gorge named after coyotes? There must be another way. If there's one thing to be thankful for, it is the prominence of fir trees. We will not have to endlessly forage for scraps of firewood.

Our midday stop is canceled. Alvah passes by, and I stop him briefly. "Why cross today? Couldn't we wait and cross when the weather is better?"

He tips his head forward and rain streams from the brim. "No, we can't do that. The scouts say that the canyon which empties into the Grande Ronde on the south side of the river increases the danger of getting swept away by flash flooding. No, we need to get to the north side of the river before we rest."

I don't know how, given the tumultuous jostling of the wagon wheels and the worry about a canyon full of coyotes, but somehow, exhaustion overtakes me. I awaken to the sounds of people shouting, and lightning cracks overhead. I glance at Agapito and I am surprised to see that his eyes are open. He speaks, and I'm overwhelmed by the fact that I can understand his words. He says, "I believe we have reached the Grande Ronde, *querida*."

My hands reach to gather my frizzy hair which has freed itself during my long nap, and I blurt, "I'm so glad, Agapito." Let him think I'm glad to reach the river, but rather, it is the sound of his voice that warms my heart and curls my toes.

"Sounds like many wagons have crossed. I should help them."

A voice near my feet surprises me. "Dolly is scared."

I had forgotten that Dahlia Jane was in the wagon with us today. It amazes me how she can play by herself with very little to entertain her for such long stretches of time. Agapito says, "Would Dolly like to ride up here with me, *amorcita*?"

The child says, "Yes. Me too."

When Dahlia Jane and her little one are comfortably seated beside Agapito, I point to his bandages and warn her to be careful of his injury. Then, I sigh and lament, "How many rivers have we crossed, and how many more are there?"

"My brain is too scrambled to count. Grande Ronde is usually easy, but it sounds like they are having trouble with it today."

"Is it because of the rain?"

"Sometimes places that are not used to getting a lot of rain are not built to handle it."

Looking through the opening at the front of the wagon reminds me of windows and civilization. I tell Agapito about the Appleyard's wagon, and the four men supervising its passage. "There's Dembi Koofai, and Arikta, of course, and Alvah on the opposite bank. Who is the fourth man?" I squint. "Why, look at that. It's Ross McAdams. He's helping." Is it pride I feel, or surprise? Did he volunteer, or was he asked to help?

"That means we are next."

A loud crack of thunder splits the airwaves. I say, "The sooner the better. Are you ready?"

He lifts his head and looks down at his body. "My arms and legs are tied. I am all strapped down. So, I am as ready as I am going to get."

The whip cracks nearby, and I recognize Christopher's voice when he hollers, "Hiya!" The team of oxen pulls us into the river. I wonder whether it is deep enough that the oxen will have to swim, or whether the wheels will reach the bottom all the way across.

Agapito says, "It is not deep, but the current is strong when it rains."

I'm glad when the wagon makes it safely across, and then I move to watch our wagon from the opening in the back.

Our weathered rig makes its way into the water. Stillman cracks the whip beside Scrapple and the wheels descend into the water. In little more than a blink, the river rises. I've never witnessed anything like it. The wagon wobbles in the middle of the river.

I turn my head and look upstream. A large object tumbles though the rough water. It looks like a beast. Perhaps it's a moose, or maybe a buffalo. I look back to the wagon. Will they collide? It can't be. I can't help but scream. It's such a helpless feeling to watch a disaster unfold and be powerless to stop it.

A buffalo carcass smashes into our wagon, busting it into pieces upon impact, sweeping everything we own down the river. Boards and splinters bob and tumble in the current.

My eyes search for Stillman, and I can't see him in the swirling waters, amongst the debris. Dembi Koofai points, and shouts. "I see him." The Shoshone scout jumps into the water and splashes about. I know he can swim. My heart skips a beat. Then, I can't see Stillman or Dembi Koofai.

Ross's long legs splash along the riverbank. I must stick my head through the opening to see the periphery. Ross stops suddenly, and throws a rope that I hadn't noticed he was carrying. I can't help but gasp as he pulls the rope taught, dragging Dembi Koofai and Stillman to the surface. As he pulls them safely to land, panic overwhelms me. With my hands at my temples, I look down at the floorboards. We've lost everything.

More importantly, where are Andrew and Rose?

Sunday, September 22

It was a fitful night of howling winds and vexing nightmares. The dawn of a new day doesn't bring clarity or freshness. What will we do now? Absent-mindedly, I poke the blanket covering Agapito beneath his body, hoping to keep him warm.

We've lost most of the things we brought with us. I was so concerned about other mothers' sons that I overlooked the safety of my own children. After the disaster, I was grateful to Arikta for running to me with the news that Andrew and Rose had crossed the river with Alvah Nye's wagon before we did. Knowing my children are safe is a huge relief, but even if others find fault in it, I can't help looking after the orphans—Ross, Stillman, and the scouts—even if they are fully grown. What if something had happened to me? I'd like to think that somebody else's mother would look out for my children, as well as her own.

Last night, Hollis and Charlotte made room for Rose in their wagon. Stillman and Andrew slept under the wagon master's awning, crowding the scouts, and Dahlia Jane stayed with me. Christopher slept with Honey and her puppy in Alvah Nye's wagon.

I stroke Agapito's dark hair and feel a tug at the hem of my trousers. Dahlia Jane says, "Mama, what happens when a turtle loses its shell?" Before I can answer, she says, "I don't want to be a turtle anymore. Can't we live in a real house?"

Agapito's warm voice reassures the child, but surprises me. "It will not be long, now, *amorcita*. You must be patient. Soon, you will reach your new home, and someday you will forget all about turtles."

It was all she needed to hear. Sometimes children are hard to convince, and other times, they're easy to reassure with vague suggestions. I tell Agapito we'll be back shortly. On the way back from tempting snakes, Dahlia Jane returns to Cobb's wagon. I like to watch her play with Bess and Joe, but I'm in a hurry to return to Agapito's side.

Though I've been sympathetic to the point of view that we should travel on Sundays, I'm glad for a day off. Hopefully, Agapito will recover better without being tied to a board and bounced in a rickety wagon all day. Thankfully, the weather has improved. It would be nice to see if we can get Agapito out of that wagon for at least a few hours.

Hollis and Charlotte step from the wagon master's rig as I return. In response to my inquiry, Hollis says, "He hasn't changed, but he should start to improve now."

I'd like to hear the optimism in his tone. When Hollis says that Agapito should start to get better, his voice doesn't sound reassuring. I say, "You're worried about him, aren't you?"

Hollis clears his throat and grumbles. "A doctor always worries about his patients, Dorcas. He seems stronger, but I'd like to see him move his hands and feet."

When Hollis and Charlotte are gone, I wait a minute before climbing back into the wagon, gathering my thoughts as I wrangle my wild and frizzy hair. Sometimes, it is hard to maintain good cheer in the face of adversity, but times such as these require strength, not weakness. I fill my lungs with fresh air and climb back into the wagon.

Agapito frowns at me. "I heard. Hollis does not think I will ever walk again, does he? I cannot live like this. I must move my arms and legs."

"I don't want to hear it, Agapito. Remember what you told Dahlia Jane? You must be patient. I'm sure you'll recover soon and forget all about your injuries." I sit beside him and run my fingers through his hair. I've gotten used to coddling him when he's asleep or unconscious, but generally don't touch him when he's awake. With a hand on his chin, I turn his head toward me. "I have a confession to make." I close my eyes and then open them when I say his name. "I love you, Agapito. I want to spend the rest of our lives together. You don't have to marry me. I respect your promise to Merced. I don't care what anybody thinks. Where you go, I will go. When you return to Independence, we'll go with you. I'll tend the wagon and reassure the passengers while you ramrod the operation. Our lives will be a never-ending adventure. I'll make lemon scones every day. Oh, listen to me, blathering on."

His eyes look away from mine, and he says, "No, that will never do, Dorcas. I am a man and I do not want to be a burden. I can not think of such things."

Our conversation is interrupted. I'm aware of the sound of bellowing oxen. Tools slap the sides of moving wagons, and I'm surprised. It is Sunday. We are laying by. Why are wagons moving? Arikta and Dembi Koofai climb into the wagon. Arikta says, "We are taking him outside."

Dembi Koofai says, "He needs to go for a swim."

Arikta pinches his nose and says, "Agapito would not forgive us if we allowed him to smell bad."

My lips sputter. "What about his wound?"

"We will be careful."

I follow them from the wagon and stop without taking a step. Alvah Nye has parked his wagon between the wagon master's rig and Cobb's. The frontiersman stands with his right arm gesturing toward the wagon.

I suck in a quick breath and cover my mouth with a hand. What is Alvah doing?

In his low voice, he says, "I want you and your family to have my wagon."

My mouth feels dry. I try to voice a protest, but all I can manage to say is, "Oh, Alvah" before he interrupts me.

He raises his voice. "You need it more than I do. Besides, I'm with *them* now." He nods toward the scouts. "I wasn't meant to be a farmer. This work suits me better."

I step toward Alvah and rest my forehead on his shoulder. What can I say to the man to express my gratitude?

Galusha Gains stomps up and swears. Then he says to Alvah, "You're too young, can't hunt, and you make stupid decisions. It's your fault that wagon wrecked in the river yesterday. We need a *man* in charge of this wagon train, not some wet-behind-the-ears whippersnapper."

Alvah doesn't have a chance to defend him. The words snap from my mouth quickly. "Nonsense, Galusha. Nobody could have predicted a dead buffalo in the river. And look across the Grande Ronde. What if we had camped there instead? Everything is underwater over there."

Captain Meadows steps forward. "That's right. I agree with Mrs. Moon. We already voted on the Alvah Nye matter. It is settled." Arikta and Dembi Koofai have finished propping Agapito into place beside a small campfire, and make their way quickly to Alvah Nye's side, as if protecting him from Galusha's challenge. Captain Meadows continues, "What we haven't settled is the matter of Ross McAdams, cattle rustler, horse thief, and member of a notorious gang of outlaws. A week ago, we placed him on probation. Now, the time has come to decide his fate."

As if to add to his defense, I say, "Yesterday, Ross saved Stillman and Dembi Koofai from the river. If he hadn't stepped forward, they could have drowned. He is no longer an outlaw. Now, he is a hero."

Galusha Gains disagrees. "That's what he wants you to think. You trust him. Let your guard down. Then, when you least expect it. Pow." Galusha smacks his right fist into the open palm of his left hand. "Don't come crying to me when he robs you all blind."

Frida Lett, who never says anything, emerges from the crowd. I didn't think she spoke any English. "Vee like heem. Vee vant to keep heem."

Captain Meadows is evidently not in the mood for a lengthy debate. "Let's vote. Those men who want to hang him to the left. If you want to forgive him, step to the right."

He may have intended that only men vote, but I step forward, take Frida's arm, and step off to the right. Galusha Gains sneers at us and steps to the left. Samuel Grosvenor and Horace Blocker follow him, and the rest of our fellow travelers are frozen in place. Did they forget that they would have to decide Ross's fate?

Landon Young and Sully Pierce join Galusha, Samuel, and Horace. I'm grateful when Captain Meadows moves toward Frida and me, until he whispers, "Only men vote."

"Not today, Captain." I frown as Oona Reid joins those who wish to see Ross hang, and Miranda Knox follows her. My family joins me and I whisper to Captain Meadows. "Today, women and children vote too."

I'm disappointed, but not surprised, when my friends from home, Addie and Esther, step to the left. But I am grateful when Stillman, Hollis, Charlotte, Alvah, Arikta, and Dembi Koofai join me.

Galusha gripes, "The crew don't get to vote."

Bobby and Wayne—the best friends and worst enemies—split their votes.

Today, mercy and forgiveness prevail. A majority of two-thirds to one has determined that, for Ross McAdams, justice means a chance for redemption. Every man, woman, and child, including newborn babes in arms, have voted with their presence, except for Agapito. I look over at the man seated beneath the awning beside a crackling fire. Perhaps it is just my imagination. I'd swear there is a twinkle of pride in his eyes.

What if the vote had come down to a tie? Would Agapito have been forced to tip the scales in one direction or the other?

Would Agapito have chosen mercy for the man who shot him?

Monday, September 23

I MUST BE OUT of my mind.

What was I thinking, telling Agapito that we would travel back to Independence and make the trip again next year? This journey has been plagued by one disaster after another. We've all been touched by the tragic loss of so many lives. Poor little Dahlia Jane just wants a permanent home. Yet, despite the many hardships, I can't help thinking of our journey as a marvelous adventure. Even now.

I think of men like Lucky and his son, Alvah Nye. Neither one belongs tethered to a fixed destination, but who ever heard of a woman who felt the same way? We're supposed to want domestic bliss, a stable home, and a welcoming hearth. I enjoy cooking, but to me, freedom is the wind blowing through my hair, riding a fast horse, and gazing at a landscape I've never seen before. It's not just the demands of love and the desire to follow Agapito wherever he goes that gives me pause. I wonder, does love tie people down, or set them free? Couldn't lovers enjoy freedom together?

I guess we didn't lose everything when our ship sank. It may seem ridiculous, but since the prairie schooner met its demise in water, I tend to think of it as a shipwreck. I'm grateful for everyone's safety, but it pains me to think of Scrapple, the other drowned oxen, and our chickens that perished in the disaster. I should be more concerned about the loss of our possessions, especially our food and money, though we didn't have much left of either. We have the clothes on our backs. Stillman had the Jew's harp and the letter I wrote to him in his pocket. Rose was wearing the trinkets that Snarling Wolf gave her. Before crossing, Andrew carried the back issues of *The Rolling Home Times* to Alvah Nye's wagon. Christopher carried Larkin's watch. Dahlia Jane had Dolly with her. I have Larkin's hat, trousers, rifle, and revolver, but it has been a long time since I thought of them as anything but mine. And I have the mane comb I bought from Muddy George. Other than that, we lost everything.

Yesterday, the scouts said Agapito needed fresh air rather than confinement. This morning, they peeled the canvas bonnet from the ribs, fashioned a backrest in the wagon bed, and tied Agapito in a seated position. Instead of sitting beside him, I walk along beside the rig. It feels good to stretch my legs, and I'm glad not to burden the oxen needlessly as they drag their cargo up one mountain after another.

When Agapito is in the mood to talk, he chatters cheerfully. I listen, smile, and wish for his recovery. When he grows tired and sits quietly, my mind wanders. I quiz myself and try to decide which moments are my most treasured memories. I'll never forget standing alone on Independence Rock. Looking back, there's no denying that I've been in love with Agapito since we rode together to the top of Scotts Bluff. Maybe the moment I heard his voice on the streets of Independence stands out.

What is your dream? I remember being confused when Agapito asked me that question. I never knew that traveling through a desolate wilderness would suit me so completely. Though a couple of days' sojourn would be welcome, I'll miss the trail when our journey ends. Is it my ideal to journey endlessly, helping people pursue their dreams?

My thoughts return again to horses. Wild horses. I don't want to live in a town, or spend my days beneath a roof. I fantasize a busy ranch, with fields of horses, a bunkhouse full of cowboys, and jagged mountains dotted with conifers. Could I own and manage a spread like that? Imagine a woman running such an enterprise.

How frivolous to think of such things after having lost everything. Traipsing through the gorgeous Blue Mountains makes one prone to irrational thoughts.

We're exhausted when we reach Meacham Creek. After we settle in and complete the day's chores, folks gather at The Hub.

Andrew's account of Ross's pardon raises questions others hadn't thought of. What will become of the stock rescued from the outlaw's hideout? I'd love to own Larry Pritchard's brother's cremello, Señorita. What about Muddy George's lone surviving donkey, and Miner Trudgeon's gold sniffing mule? Who wouldn't want a creature with such a gift? It wouldn't be possible to find the rightful heirs or owners of the stolen stock. And what about Boss Wheel's fortune? According to Andrew's interviews, every dollar the man ever made was sewn into his capote.

Captain Meadows says, "As partners in this enterprise, unexpected gains should be split amongst us." Most folks agree, but the fact is, nobody knows what happened to Boss Wheel's money. I try to concentrate, but my memory becomes foggy when I think about the battle's aftermath. So much happened in a short time. Did the bank notes end up in the fire? Did the coins get kicked into a dark corner of the cave? I can't remember anybody scurrying to collect the money. Maybe those who buried the dead had an opportunity. If somebody knows, nobody's saying.

Galusha Gains says, "Let's search everybody's wagon. Then, we'll know who is holding out on us."

Something about Galusha, Samuel, and Horace brings out the worst in me. "What if Boss Wheel's life savings was in my wagon? What then? Maybe you should search the bottom of the Grande Ronde river."

Galusha calls me a name I shall not repeat, but I would confess to his accusation of impertinence. He says, "When we sell the stock in Oregon City, she gets nothing since her share is underwater."

Alvah says, "Mrs. Moon is entitled to the same as everyone else, if you are splitting it evenly. But what about Boss Wheel's family? If he saved a fortune, aren't his children entitled to benefit?"

Samuel scoffs, "Children? You mean *breeds*, don't you?

Galusha adds, "What would they need money for?"

Captain Meadows frowns. "I hadn't thought of that. Shame on me. Of course, the man's heirs are entitled to his estate."

Galusha says, "How would they ever know? I'll never tell 'em. You can be sure of that."

I say, "Yesterday you wanted to hang a guy for stealing. Today you want to take what doesn't belong to you."

Captain Meadows says, "She's right. If anybody wants to confess and turn over the money, let me know. If anyone has information about Boss Wheel's savings, tell me. The scouts can take the money to his family when they pass through next year. As for the stolen stock, everyone over eighteen will share in the proceeds, except for Ross McAdams."

Galusha points at Cobb. "Even them?"

Captain Meadows says, "Everyone means everyone. This matter is settled."

Tuesday, September 24

"*Mira, querida.*" Agapito lifts his leg and turns his foot. He hasn't lifted his leg high, or turned his foot fast, but it's encouraging.

I open my mouth with profuse optimism in mind, and hear Dahlia Jane's voice, instead. I step back and let her speak to him. She sounds like a child pretending to be an adult. "Look at you. That's great. Now you can play with me, *amorcita.*"

"Ah, you must call me *amorcito*, remember? I should like very much to run and play with you, but my legs are not strong enough yet. They only have a little wiggle in them, you see?"

"How about your fingers and arms? Do they have any wiggle in them?"

He strains his face, pinches his lips together, and commands his arms to move. "How about that, child? I could almost tickle you, yes?"

Dahlia Jane squeals with delight. It's almost as if she can feel his fingers tickling her ribs. "That's very good, Pito."

"I think so too." The man looks up at me with wide eyes and an earnest grin. He's clearly relieved. "I was beginning to think my arms and legs had gone to sleep and would never wake up again."

Dahlia Jane wags a finger at him. "Don't let anybody shoot you anymore, okay?"

Agapito's eyebrows dance with amusement as he responds. "That is good advice. I shall insist that nobody ever shoot me again. Thank you, Dahlia Jane." He turns his head back toward me. "It is getting late, *querida*. Why are we not moving?"

"It snowed last night. Hunting parties went out at dawn. Everyone is short on food, and Alvah thinks there is a good chance of finding game in these mountains. With a little snow on the ground, they hope to see tracks. We are told today will be a short march to Emigrant Springs. If they're not back by ten, we'll head off without them, and they'll catch up when they can."

My stomach growls, and I'm not the only one that hears it. Agapito looks at me from the corner of his eye, but he doesn't say anything.

We're interrupted by Hollis and Charlotte. The doctor is pleased to see Agapito's progress. "There's no telling what the human body will do. Sometimes, it takes a little while before a body can figure out how to move after a trauma. Maybe it is a miracle."

Agapito says, "Maybe it was the fresh air. Is it too much trouble to take the bonnet down again today?"

The doctor hems and haws. "Today is not as warm as yesterday. I don't want you to catch a chill."

Agapito is disappointed but doesn't challenge the doctor's judgment.

When Hollis and Charlotte leave, Dahlia Jane goes with them. Later, as Stillman, Andrew, and Christopher hitch up the oxen, I help Agapito back into a sitting position and tie him loosely in place. I ask, "Are you comfortable," as I drape a warm blanket over him.

He confirms that he is. I place my hands on his cheeks, tip his head back, and gently kiss his lips. My eyes reopen just before he opens his eyes.

Agapito smiles. It isn't the playful smile I'm used to seeing. There's a deep sincerity to his expression, and it remains on his face despite the playful words he says. "I never imagined being a prisoner would feel like this."

"Good Heavens, Agapito. I'm sorry we must tie you up. I don't think I have the strength to keep you from being pitched from stem to stern."

"I understand. Do not worry. Thank you for taking such good care of me. I am grateful."

I sit beside him, cross my legs and arms. "Have you thought about what I said the other day?"

He nods.

"I should have waited until you were feeling better to tell you those things."

"I was glad to hear what you said."

"Love is just love. It doesn't have to be complicated, does it? You do not have to marry me to love me, Agapito. Maybe if we lived in a city or town, but on the frontier, who is to care?"

His head turns away from me and his voice trails off as he says, "If I survive, we can speak of the future then."

I don't want to think about the possibility that he will not survive. Whether we've got decades yet to live or only hours, I don't want to wait any longer. Can't he see that we are meant to be together?

There's a rap on the back of the wagon. Confound the interruption.

It is surprising to see Ross. He sits beside me when I invite him to board. It doesn't take him long to explain what's on his mind. I've seen the hangdog look on him so often, it's quite a contrast to see enthusiasm. His rosy cheeks are even redder than normal. He licks his lips, puffs his chest, and says, "You know that little blond girl, Berta? I asked her to marry me, and she said yes. Her mother gave her blessing, and we want to get married on Saturday. It's all because of you, Dorcas. I did exactly what you said."

With my hand on my chest, just beneath my chin, I say, "Me? Good Heavens, Ross. Whatever do you mean?" I turn slightly toward him, look back at Agapito, who looks amused, and then back at the young man.

"Yes, you told me how to treat a lady. To ask first, and stuff. Berta loves it."

"But, Ross. You've only known her a week. Just ten days ago, you thought you wanted hundreds of women, not just one."

"I know. I was wrong. Now I know. Now I understand. If it weren't for you, I would have messed it up. Do you think Captain Meadows will marry us?"

I take my hat off, scratch my scalp and place it back on my head. "I don't know. If Frida approves, and Berta says yes, how could Captain Meadows say no?"

"That's what I thought. But what if he does? Can anybody else do it? We want it to be official. Legal like, and all."

Agapito says, "Boss Wheel married people sometimes. So, I guess wagon masters are permitted to marry people outside of the States."

"Aren't you the wagon master now, officially?"

Agapito grins, says to Ross, "Yes, I suppose I am," and winks at me. "You understand marriage is a serious commitment, *hombre*? Until death do we part. Will you love Berta that long?"

The youth nods furiously. "I swear, I will."

Wednesday, September 25

We're fortunate that Old Man Winter has shown restraint, leaving us only an inch of snow rather than an early blizzard. Yet, it is cold enough to freeze water left in the bucket overnight. Again, we wait for hunters, and a late departure before making our daily journey.

Today, a hardy cheer greets the triumphant hunters when they return, mid-morning. A chant echoes across camp: "Hip, hip, hooray." A parade of jubilant children and appreciative parents follow the men to The Hub. Our patience is rewarded with a couple of elk and a large deer, but instead of cooking them immediately, they are hastily butchered and set aside for the evening.

During the day, as we make our long descent from Crawford Hill, I think about Ross's bombshell news. To think, just a day after winning a pardon, the young man is engaged, to Berta, no less, a pretty girl I once envied as if she were a rival. Ross thinks that my advice helped him woo her, but I bet Berta's love will ultimately save him. It won't be the first or last time a good woman reformed a troubled man.

But what about Agapito? Yesterday, I was optimistic that he was on the mend. This morning, I am not so sure. He confirmed that he heard my proposition, and he said he was glad. I would have preferred to know that he felt the same way I do. Instead, he said, "If I survive, we can speak of the future then." Most men can't do or think about two things at the same time. Maybe they don't work that way. In contrast, I seem to be capable of worrying about a dozen things, all at once. If it weren't for Agapito's injury, I would probably worry even more about running out of food. Rather than relying on the hunters, I would join them.

Our generous young leader, Alvah Nye, is a hero. I am eternally grateful to him for the use of his wagon, and the gift of his provisions. If Boss Wheel were still alive, I think he himself would be impressed to see Alvah's patient, steadfast management of our expedition. Sometimes, it is hard to believe the man is only twenty years old. And, thank Heaven he is wise enough to know when to listen to the experienced scouts rather than assume he knows what's best without their counsel. Now, Alvah and the hunters have brought in meat. I've been skipping meals to make sure there's enough food for the children, but my mouth waters at the thought of an elk roast.

As the afternoon wears on, Agapito's condition worsens. At first, I think it is just a matter of absent-mindedness when he talks about reaching the Platte River at the end of the day. It's been months since we followed that waterway. "You mean the Umatilla River, don't you, Agapito. Only, we are told tonight we'll have a dry camp. Tomorrow we will reach the Umatilla River."

He sighs. "Old Wheel should push us faster. We could reach the river today." Then he starts talking about his mother, converts to Spanish, and slurs his words. I place the back of my hand on his forehead and worry that he has contracted a fever.

I tell Agapito that I will be back in a couple of minutes, and he babbles on as if unaware that I'm speaking to him. When I return with Charlotte, Rose follows, leaving Hollis with their oxen. Most women have become adept at driving the wagons, but Charlotte is not one of them. It occurs to me that Rose has been spending a lot of time with Charlotte since Snarling Wolf's tragic murder.

While examining Agapito, Charlotte speaks as if she were a doctor. She monitors his pulse, smells his breath, looks into his mouth, feels his forehead, looks into his eyes and notes the mottled patchiness of his skin. The patient normally has a healthy pallor and uniform complexion. Charlotte grumbles. "This reminds me of Jennie."

I snap at Charlotte, "What? How can it be? Jennie died of childbed fever, how could Agapito have *that*?"

Charlotte answers, "This sometimes happens to men after surgeries, Dorcas, only we don't call it by the same name. We call it *corruption*. It is very difficult to cure."

Rose says, "Tea will help."

Charlotte shrugs. "Maybe so. Couldn't hurt."

"Do you have any honey in your wagon?"

Charlotte confirms that she does and promises to return with some. When she's gone, Rose whispers, "Janey says to make sage tea with honey. Make him drink as much of it as he can stand."

"Janey? You mean Sacagawea? Is she here now?"

"Not anymore, Mama. She left when you said her name."

Good Heavens. Agapito's life is in danger and we're depending on a ghost to prescribe treatments. What does Martha Washington advise? I suppose if Charlotte doesn't object to Rose's suggestion, what can it hurt?

"Mama, you have that look on your face again."

"What?" I'm startled by Rose, interrupting my thoughts. "What face?"

"The face you make when you don't believe me. I thought you were finally coming to accept the fact that I can talk to dead people. But it isn't true, is it? You still aren't convinced. What's it going to take?" She shakes her head and her stringy hair sways with the movement of her head. She seems different than she used to, though. Rather than disgust, she seems disappointed. Much as I disliked the feeling that she was disgusted with me, her disappointment now hurts more than her anger used to.

I say, "I'm sorry, Rose. I'm still learning to understand. Give me time."

I'm not used to seeing Rose display an amused expression. It is as if she's saying that time won't change a thing.

When Charlotte returns, Rose mixes honey into water. Then she pulls a handful of gray powder from her pocket and sprinkles it into the tumbler.

I say, "Doesn't tea need to be hot?"

Rose says, "It might taste better, but it isn't necessary. He can drink this now."

"That's good. I don't imagine we can stop the wagons to heat a cup of tea."

As Charlotte departs, she says, "Try not to worry, dear. I'll send Hollis by when we make camp."

Thursday, September 26

We enjoyed a rich repast last night, and though it is an unusual breakfast, we feasted on elk again this morning. I'm glad to have satiated our hunger, but it is hard to enjoy such a luxury while Agapito's life is in danger.

Thinking back to when Jennie wasted away to nothing, and then perished, just after the birth of her beautiful baby girl, makes me worry that Agapito will die, just as she did. What will I do if that happens? Instead of letting myself think of that, I always distract myself by diverting my thoughts. I've accepted a lot of loss, particularly on this expedition, but I'm not sure that I could face up to losing him.

Hollis and Charlotte agree that many people survive the corruption. They warn that we could be forced to wait for several days before we know if he will make it.

When we are alone, Rose tells me that it doesn't matter whether I believe in ghosts, but that I must allow her to administer the strange tea she brews. Recalling Galusha and Samuel's insistent accusation that Rose is a witch, I can't help but worry what they will think if they find out that Rose is stirring up potions. I prepare to explain that Rose is studying medicinal herbs, and that Charlotte is teaching her. Hopefully, if Hollis and Charlotte endorse her, Rose can escape the naysayers, should they challenge her again. Then again, who cares what they think? It's not like they could burn her at the stake. People don't do such things to suspected witches anymore.

So, what does it matter? As long as Agapito isn't harmed by the remedy, why not let him drink it? Who knows, if Rose turns out to be right, it could even save his life. Unfortunately, he doesn't seem to enjoy consuming the tea. It's impossible to make sense of the garbled words Agapito attempts to mumble, but the expression on his face makes it clear that he doesn't like the beverage. I take a taste to see how bad it is, but I don't mind it. "That's not bad, Rose. Have you tried it?"

She nods. "I don't like the taste of honey, but I like sage."

"Do you think Agapito might like the honey and sage better if you put it in coffee instead of serving it as tea?"

Rose shrugs. "He might. As long as he gets the honey and sage. It doesn't matter about the coffee."

"Let's give it a try."

Though we're sitting with Agapito and his eyes are open, he doesn't seem to be listening. He looks sort of like Rose does when she communicates with ghosts, except for the occasional wince, and sometimes, beads of sweat appear on his brow.

I've had few chances to talk to Rose since her husband's death, and I've been curious about their marriage. Talking with Rose is sometimes a challenge. Instead of asking what I'd really like to know, I say, "Did you like being married?"

Her head jerks toward me. "Why do you ask?"

"I'm just curious, dear." What I'd really like to know is whether she is with child, not that I've seen the slightest indication. They weren't married long, perhaps it was six weeks, but certainly that would be long enough. Perhaps another approach would work. "Do you think you'd like to get married again someday?" She shrugs but doesn't verbalize a response. I can't restrain myself any longer. "Were you and Snarling Wolf intimate, dear?"

Rose's eyes roll. She doesn't answer my question. Instead she says, "When the scouts return to Independence, I'm going with them. I'm going to Washakie's village. If Sees Through Clouds wants me to be his woman, I will. In addition to being a seer, I want to be a healer. Charlotte knows a lot, and I'm learning everything I can from her, and from Hollis. I know you don't want to hear it, but Janey also knows many things about herbal remedies."

I consider telling Rose about the proposition I made to Agapito. What would she think if I told her we might also return to the trail next year? Her temper is mighty unpredictable. I decide to wait until Agapito regains his health and see what he thinks of my offer. "I see. Why are you compelled to go there?"

"Why does anybody do anything, Mama? Sees Through Clouds understands me. Washakie accepts me."

"Have you talked to Dembi Koofai about this?"

"No. What's he got to do with me?"

"He is a Shoshone." I picture the scout with the scorpion's pincers clamped onto his chest when we camped with Washakie at the Birthing Stone. "He could tell you what it is like to live with his people."

"I already know that, Mama."

Should I leave it at that? I decide to inquire further. "How, dear? How could you know that?"

"Sees Through Clouds showed me his memories. Everything that happened to him and his family since he was born. You were there, Mama. You saw us sharing memories. Have you already forgotten?"

Is that what they were doing? I shudder at the recollection. It felt creepy being near them, and I just wanted to get her away from that man. "I have not forgotten. How old is Sees Through Clouds, Rose?"

Rose is clearly disgusted by my question. "Pshaw," she exclaims. "Who cares? Why does everybody care so much about that? It doesn't matter how old we are, but rather, how our spirits mingle. Don't you see?"

"I'm not sure, honey." I search for something more to say, but can't find the words.

"Maybe someday you'll understand. You don't catch on very quickly."

The last time we had a conversation like this, it ended poorly. I believe she called me a *dolt* or a *dorbug*. That was months ago. I'm determined not to repeat whatever mistake I made that day. I tap her forearm, and say, "Be patient with me, dear. Some people learn slower than others."

I shall have to wait to find out whether Rose is with child. I must admit that I hope she is not. Her spirit may be wise, but she is so young. I'd like for her to be older, and more able to cope with the physical world.

The wagons circle, ending our conversation, and we meet a new waterway, the Umatilla River.

Friday, September 27

As the wagon master's conveyance rolls through the afternoon, Agapito sleeps, as he has most of the day. I'm not sure whether there's a difference between sleeping and being unconscious, but I spend most of the day dabbing him with a moist cloth and watching the river as we pass it by. It's hard to remember that September is almost over when the sun shines all day, and there's no shade. If it weren't for tending Agapito, I'd be walking away the miles, and sweating along with everybody else. It's hard to comprehend how it can get so cold at night, and yet be so warm in the afternoon.

When Ross steps up into the wagon, I must admit that I'm grateful for the diversion. I'm looking forward to thinking about something other than whether the man I love will perish today.

Ross is fidgety and breathing hard. When he starts to talk, his words come fast, but he practically whispers them. "I don't know what to do." He looks at Agapito, stretched out on the board. Since we've returned to flat terrain, I haven't tied him down, though I have wedged him between quilts and pillows. "Can he hear us?"

"I don't think so, Ross. What do you mean, you don't know what to do? About what?"

He jabs his head toward me, urgently. "Being married. I'm getting married tomorrow, remember?" His back arches, and it looks like he might slither from the small barrel he's sitting on and wind up on the floor.

"Yes, I remember. Are you having second thoughts?"

He looks at me dumbly and blinks rapidly. "No, I'm not having second thoughts. I'm having a million thoughts. I can't think of anything else."

"So you still want to go through with it then?"

He pounds his knee with a fist. "Of course I want to go through with it. You've seen Berta, haven't you?" Ross smacks his forehead with the palm of his hand.

"So what's the problem? Are you nervous about the ceremony?"

"What ceremony? What do you mean? Nervous about the ceremony?"

"The part where Captain Meadows marries you and Berta."

"Oh. Why should I be nervous about that?"

"You shouldn't. When he asks you a question and then stops talking, if you still want to get married, you say, 'I do.' That's about it. It doesn't get too fancy out here on the frontier."

His face reddens, his head tips back, and the tendons in his flexed neck threaten to burst through his skin. "I don't care about that part." He gulps hard, and it seems painful. "What do I do on my wedding *night*? How do I... ugh. Why am I talking to *you* about *this*?"

What does it say about me that I find his discomfort so entertaining? "Is that what's troubling you? Do you know how that works? I presume somebody has explained it to you, your brothers maybe?"

"Ah, Hell. I guess I know the..." he waves his open hand back and forth through the air, as if searching for a euphemism, "mechanics of the situation." He exhales and slumps. "But I don't know the first thing about how to get from the first step to the last step, if you know what I mean."

"Then don't pretend you do, Ross. Berta probably doesn't either. Just tell her it's your first time. Ask her for permission every step of the way. Tell her you reckon you'll figure it out together. Sure, you'll be nervous at first, but nature has a way of working this out. She'll probably be nervous too, so just be gentle. Remember that you love her."

Russ gulps a breath of air. "Okay, alright. Okay. So what do I do about her family? They're gonna *know*, aren't they? How are we supposed to be married with all of them right there and everything? Heck, this is complicated. Isn't it noisy? And... bumpy? What do I do about that?"

"Well, Ross. Here's what you do. Get yourself a nice, clean blanket, tell your new family that you want to spend some time alone with your wife, and go find yourself a secluded spot by the river. That way you don't have to be noisy and bumpy with them right there. If the weather is bad, you might need to wait for the next night."

I glance at Agapito. His eyes are closed, but it looks like the corners of his mouth are slightly turned. His tell-tale dimple makes me wonder if he can hear our conversation.

Ross blurts, "Oh, no. I can't wait that long. I can barely stand to wait until tomorrow."

"Maybe you should try to think about something else for the rest of the day. Unless you have any other questions."

The color drains from his face. He gushes, "Thank you, Dorcas. I feel so much better." His mouth hangs open for a moment. "If it weren't for you, I'm sure I'd a messed it all up. I swear."

I nod gently to reassure him and change the subject. "What do you think about the mystery of Boss Wheel's fortune?"

Ross blinks quickly as if trying to forget about Berta for a minute. "Oh, the wagon master with the heavy capote that The Viper killed?" He pauses briefly, then speaks quickly enough that I can tell he's given the subject some thought. "I think that husky, blond haired kid, Garland, scooped up the wagon master's fortune. That is, unless you think the new wagon master could have done it. What's his name again?"

"Do you mean Alvah? Alvah Nye?"

"Yeah, that's the one."

I shake my head, "I don't think I lost sight of him. Remember, he rode back to get a wagon for Agapito, and then he rode with you, me, and Rose up Birch Creek to your cabin. Besides, he's nearly the last one I would suspect."

Ross says, "You're the last one I would suspect." He chuckles. "It wasn't you, was it?"

I frown and shake my head. "Of course not."

He continues, "Think about it. Try to picture it. Remember when Rose grabbed that giant, golden rattler in her bare hands, and dropped it in the fire. Everyone was mesmerized by that, but that Garland was closest to the cash, wasn't he? Maybe he didn't have time to pocket the silver, but he could have stashed the paper in his pants, mighty fast."

"I remember rushing to Agapito's side at the mouth of the cave. I thought he was dead, but then he moved." I glance at Agapito again. I'm relieved to see his chest rise and fall. His eyes are still closed. I turn back toward Ross and say, "Rose and Garland passed by me, and then sat together outside." I try to envision the lad. Could his trousers have been filled with Boss Wheel's heavy coinage? It's not impossible. "I'd be surprised if Garland did that. Who else had an opportunity? Hm. Do you know who buried your brothers?"

"Somebody buried them? Why would they do that? Mad as everyone was, I thought you'd all let the wolves and vultures eat 'em."

I can't help but grimace to think of it.

Ross shrugs. "Guess they had it coming. Didn't deserve any better. But I hate thinking of them being devoured. You think somebody buried Lennox, Leon, and Sloan?"

"I do." The kid has a stupid look on his face. He's truly dumbfounded that somebody would even think of tending to his brothers after all they've done. But who could have dug those graves? "Oh, I just remembered something. Do you remember Landon Young? He's the one whose sister lost her husband and wagon last year. Sarah Terwilliger. Perhaps Landon could have scooped up Boss Wheel's cash. Maybe he felt entitled to it. Do you remember who else came back with Alvah Nye and the wagon?"

Ross's legs which had been tightly drawn together, relax and part, and he bumps a knee on the corner of a wooden carton. He seems much more at ease now, and doesn't acknowledge pain in his kneecap. Ross answers, "Just the doctor. How about him?"

"Well, I could see him burying your brothers, but I couldn't imagine him taking Boss Wheel's money and not mentioning it. Besides, that would be a lot of work for Hollis to do on his own, and he's not a young man."

Ross raises his eyebrows and says, "What about the scouts?"

"That's a thought. They could have buried your brothers. I think Arikta would have mentioned picking up the money. Dembi Koofai might have gathered it, but not said anything. But, even if he did, I think he would make sure that Boss Wheel's family got the cash."

Ross gestures with open hands and says, "It *is* a mystery."

"Sure is hard to figure. Everything happened so fast. No telling what happened for sure."

Ross bites his lower lip and then says, "What if the money is just lying there. Like gold inside a mountain. Somebody's just gonna come along and find it. Imagine that. Gosh, I forgot all about getting married tomorrow."

"You sure you still want to go through with that?"

"Oh yeah." He raises his eyebrows several times in rapid succession. "You'd better believe it. More'n anything." Ross grabs and jostles the buckle on his gun belt.

Saturday, September 28

The wedding is set to commence an hour after the wagons circle, which gives most families barely enough time to tend to the stock, grease the axles, and fill the water barrels. It's not that I mind attending the celebration, though it's hard to forget that they just met.

Ross fell in love with Berta before he even saw her face. I saw the moment that it happened. She was bent at the waist hoisting a bucket of water from Burnt Creek. The young outlaw fell in love with her backside. She barely speaks English, perhaps enough to get by, and probably doesn't care about Ross's past. If Alvah Nye had paid Berta the slightest bit of attention, she might have fallen in love with him instead of Ross.

Should I have tried harder to convince Ross that he should wait a while before making such a permanent commitment as marriage? I'd like to convince myself that it had nothing to do with my fear of Berta winding up with Agapito. I suppose Ross and Berta could be madly in love and perfectly matched. Will Captain Meadows say that God has brought this couple together?

Cobb steps over from the next wagon, points to the Hub with his chin, baby Jenny in the crook of his arm, as usual. He inquires, "You going?"

"I really should." I had planned to skip it and tell everyone that I couldn't leave Agapito's side, but he just fell asleep after being awake for two and a half hours. He might still wake up and need me anyway. I stretch, yawn, and say, "Pardon me, Cobb. It seems that all of Agapito's sleeping makes me tired."

"Want to join me?

"Sure." I poke at my hair, think about the fact that I'm wearing the only clothes I own, and consider looking into a mirror. I decide that it would be better not to. What difference does it make anyway? "Don't mind if I do."

"Let's wander over, then."

I glance at Bess, Joe, and Dahlia Jane, seated beneath Cobb's wagon. "What about the children?"

"They won't even notice we're gone, and we'll be back before we know it. Prairie weddings are over quickly."

"Very well, then." I turn slightly and offer him my arm, bent at the elbow as if I were a gentleman and he were a lady. He chuckles and humors me. I sigh, and say, "What chance do they have? They're so young, and they only just met." But compared to other newlyweds, Ross and Berta are not younger than average.

Cobb says, "What difference does it make that they just met?"

"You know what it's like to be married. Don't you think it's better to know you're compatible before you make a lifelong commitment?"

"I suppose. Then again, even after you've been married for years, there's no limit to the mysteries of a woman." Cobb sniffles and adds, "Berta and The Radish remind me of Jennie and me."

What a strange thing to say. Even aside from the differences in their race, Berta and Ross don't resemble Jennie and Cobb in the slightest, and nothing about their love stories is comparable. Plus, Cobb shouldn't have called Ross, The Radish, but I decide not to mention my objections. Maybe Cobb just welcomes the opportunity to think and talk about his beloved.

Cobb continues, "Maybe it sounds crazy, but I feel like Jennie is still with me." Cobb places his right hand over his heart. "I don't just feel her in my heart. Instead, it feels *real*. Just like when she was alive, and we would look at each other. I would get so lost in her beautiful brown eyes. Just the thought of her gives me the strength to go on. Be mother and father to our children. Do what I have to do. And it doesn't make me sad to think about Jennie all of the time, it makes me happy. Sure, I wish she was still with us, but it's strange to say, it is almost like she *is* still with us. I feel it the strongest when I'm beside the wagon and when I'm taking care of our apple tree seedlings."

I look away so that Cobb will not notice the expression on my face, and say, "Do you believe in ghosts, Cobb?"

"Maybe that what would explain it. Our marriage vows say, 'til death do we part. But what if it's more than that? I still feel just as married to Jennie as I did when we were alive."

What a strange way of putting it. Does Cobb know that he said, "When *we* were alive?" Our slow, short walk to The Hub has ended. I think to inquire whether Cobb thinks he'd ever take another wife, but I don't need to ask to know the answer. Cobb is a one woman man.

The eager couple and the bride's family don't keep us waiting. Berta wears a pale pink dress, and Ross looks even more gaunt in a fresh, borrowed shirt. I wonder if it belonged to William, and when I blink, an image of the father of the bride after being gut-gored by a buffalo comes to mind. When the young man says, "I do," his loud voice jumps from deep within him. From what I'm told, most men are hesitant and many have second thoughts, whereas Ross sounds eager, like he can barely wait to get the ceremony over with.

Instead of a veil, the bride wears the tartan bandana with the words *The Radish* sewn in the corner. The very purpose of such a garment is to shield an untouched maiden from the spirits that would do her harm or thwart her happiness. Her voice sounds sweet when she answers the Captain's question. It makes me think of putting sugar, honey, and molasses in a cup of tea, and I chide myself for being judgmental. I've always frowned at the thought of sweet, pretty brides on their wedding day, ever since my childhood friend married my beloved Noah. Why should I be jealous or envious today? It's been years since Noah married Arminda, and I haven't thought of either of them in weeks, maybe even months. I should be glad that Berta has married Ross. I don't know if I could have borne witness to Berta marrying Agapito.

Cobb and I are among the first to wish the newlyweds well, and then Cobb offers me his arm for our short walk back to the wagons. I'm sure Agapito hasn't moved since we've been gone, but I'm anxious to get back just the same.

After a couple of strides, we come upon Bobby and Wayne. The two men stand a couple of feet from one another, bow legged, arms bent at their sides, their long sleeves rolled up beyond their elbows. They look like they're about to duel, though neither man is wearing a gun, and I notice that the scar on Bobby's forearm has healed to the point where it is a barely noticeable scratch, whereas the nick on Wayne's calf cannot be seen, but doesn't seem to unbalance his stance.

It's not hard to predict what's about to happen. I think back to when I first saw the young men, one in red and the other blue. I recall the times since, when the best friends have put their fists up. Goodness gracious, I wonder what's sparked their enmity today. I look at their pretty young wives, remember the time that Bobby and Wayne brawled over the question of who would become a father first, and try to judge for myself which woman's pregnancy is more advanced. I try to predict whether the blond or dark haired man will be the first to throw a punch.

Bobby says, "What business does an outlaw have marrying a fine looking woman like that?"

Wayne says, "You just want her to yourself. I saw you kiss her."

Bobby says. "You're mad." The dark-haired man jumps forward, throws the first punch, and lands his right fist on his friend's jaw.

Wayne spits, turns his head back toward Bobby and says, "Don't deny it. You always tell me my sister is ugly. I seen you ogling that German girl."

"That's crazy talk. Why you always gotta make up stuff like that?" Bobby kicks, landing a foot just beneath Wayne's rib cage, sending his friend hurtling backward to the ground.

Wayne rolls, curls his body, protectively covering his midsection, and shouts, "I've seen you. How many times you done it anyway?"

Bobby puts his head down and charges like a mad bull. "I oughta smash you so hard you never get up again."

I look at Bobby's wife, Serena. She looks like she might cry and says to me, "Why do they do this?"

What's it got to do with me? I remember the pleading look on Serena's face when Bobby and Wayne fought on the street in Independence. It occurs that she expects me to intervene again. What if I didn't? Would the bruisers work matters out themselves? Maybe if they were allowed to finish a fight, they'd quit fighting forever. But on the other hand, how many times have they brawled when I wasn't there? It never occurred to me to ask. Instead, I say to Serena, "They been into the hooch again?"

Serena frowns. Drucilla clutches Serena's arm, and says, "They can't handle their liquor. Neither one of them. They say they like drinking together, but it always turns out like this."

Serena looks at me. "Do you think Bobby's been with that..." it looks like she's trying to decide whether to say the woman's name or not, and then spits out, "Berta." Her hands caress her bloated belly. "He wouldn't do that, would he?" She looks at Drucilla. "Wayne's just saying that to make him mad, isn't he?" Serena doesn't wait for Drucilla to answer, but instead turns back to me. "Oh, won't you stop them?"

I scratch my chin and say, "I really can't stand it when men fight." The wrestling rascals tumble over one another on the dusty ground. I look at Drucilla and say, "Why don't you dump the rest of that swill they purchased at Fort Boise a couple of weeks ago, and leave these boys to me."

Cobb pushes baby Jenny toward me, and says, "Allow me, Dorcas."

I shake my head. "Nah, Cobb. It would appear that I am the law in this town, and if the drunks need to have their heads smacked together, it's up to me to do it."

Bobby's boot catches the hem of my dress when I pull him from the ground, ripping my tattered frock. Wayne's fist rips across my brow, and his foot slams into my thigh as I lift his flailing body in my left hand.

Bobby says, "Aw, not again. The girls are into our whiskey."

When their bodies sag, I drop them back to the ground and they crawl a short distance from me before getting up and scurrying off toward their wagons. Perhaps they'll get there in time to salvage a few drops of their precious liquor.

It would seem that the bride and groom failed to notice the tussle. I watch for a half a minute as the tall, reformed outlaw with a blanket beneath his arm reaches for the hand of his pretty young bride. As they stride slowly toward the Umatilla River, I shake my head. Usually, weddings make me grouchy, but today, for some reason, I feel entertained. It's certainly not ladylike to admit to such a thing, but I try to picture the couple doing what newlyweds do.

As Cobb escorts me back to the wagons, a familiar conclusion replaces the sordid images in my imagination. Love is for young people, not people my age. I remind myself that I am a middle-aged widow and a mother of four children.

Sunday, September 29

It was a long, dreadful night. Three times, I worried that Agapito had drawn his last lungful of air. Twice I raced to the Appleyard's wagon and dragged poor Hollis to check on our ailing wagon master.

The first time, Hollis said, "He should breathe more. His pulse is faint, but he's alive. I'm sorry, Dorcas. I wish there were something I could do for him."

When I retrieved Hollis again, he said, "Agapito is barely alive. I'm not sure how he's held on this long. You need to prepare yourself. He may not make it through the night."

The canvas bonnet above us slowly brightens. I'm weary but I am not compelled to close my eyes. For the hundredth time, I reach for Agapito's wrist, and place my fingers above a barely visible vein. The sun has risen, yet he remains alive.

Before breakfast, Hollis and Charlotte climb aboard and check on Agapito. After their examination, Hollis says, "I don't want you to have false hope, Dorcas. I'm surprised he's lasted this long, weak as he is. If he survives today, he just may have a chance. One way or another, today should decide it. Do you want to send for the preacher?"

As they depart, I say, "I will get him." But I'm not in any hurry. Instead, I place my lips on Agapito's brow, kiss him gently, and sit back on the barrel beside him. I sit quietly and my mind wanders. The minutes blink by and my thoughts meander, eventually drifting to Ross and Berta. Do they yet linger right beside the river? How I wish that I were beginning a life together with Agapito rather than tending to him during his final minutes.

Christopher brings me a small bowl of mush and quickly disappears. My fingers gently pry Agapito's lips apart, and I scrape several small spoonsful of warm porridge into his mouth, which he reflexively swallows. Considering that he could barely breathe overnight, it's almost a miracle that he can ingest even a small amount of nourishment.

Though I haven't sent for him yet, Captain Meadows arrives on his own, after breakfast, and takes my place on the barrel. I tell the preacher that I'll leave them alone, but when my feet hit the ground, I stand by the corner of the wagon and listen. Agapito's faith is probably of a different denomination, but hopefully the Lord will welcome the good man's heartfelt prayers. I refuse to believe that last rites are necessary, and bite my lip.

During the day, many people stop by, inquire about Agapito and offer to help. For a few minutes in the afternoon, I doze off and awaken when Rose climbs into the wagon. She carries her diary with her, and I'm surprised. As my eyes blink open, it dawns on me that somehow her journal full of secret thoughts has survived. I say, "I thought you lost that in the wreckage."

She says, "Me too. It turns out, Andrew scooped it up when he saved the newspapers." She sits quietly in the corner, occasionally scratching a couple of words onto a blank page, and after a while, I forget that she is here.

Absent-mindedly, my fingers toy with sparse hairs on Agapito's chest, while keeping a safe distance from his bandaged wound. Suddenly, I realize that he is not breathing. When Rose quietly speaks to me, I jump. "A child is with us, Mama. She's a little older than Dahlia Jane, and she's begging her father to come along. She's a beautiful girl with dark, round eyes and pretty hair."

I gasp. "Sarita." I think of the times Agapito has mentioned his little angel.

Rose whispers, "The child's mother says that she must wait."

I say, "Merced. Mercy me." Of course, if there were such a thing as ghosts, Agapito's wife would remain with him. Just recently, Cobb told me that he believes Jennie's spirit has remained nearby.

Rose says, "Merced wants Agapito to live on. She tells him to let the *chica marimacho* love him, and to forget his silly promise. She says that she is not a jealous woman, like you are. She tells him to live free of obligations to her." What difference does it make what Rose says anyway? It's not like Agapito can hear her.

Agapito sputters, coughs, and his chest heaves. It's as if he suddenly remembered to breathe again, but had almost forgotten how. If I were to believe Rose, I would think that Merced had sent him back from Heaven, which is surely where a spirit such as hers would reside.

Rose says, "Agapito is back, Mama."

"What should I do?"

"Just hold his hand. That's all he wants or needs."

How would Rose know what Agapito wants or needs? How ridiculous?

As the afternoon fades to evening, Agapito struggles to draw a breath, several times. The poor, suffering man fights to live, yet I can't stay awake. Several times, I drift off, only to fight my way back and feel guilty for having slumbered. What if Agapito needs me? What a silly notion. There's nothing that I could do for him anyway. Not even the professionals, Hollis and Charlotte, can think of anything else to do to save him.

When my mind wanders again, I think of Berta and Ross's wedding again, and the fistfight that followed it. Weddings make me sad. Usually, it takes a day or two for me to see otherwise. Today, I wonder how Ross and Berta are getting along. I know I'm responsible for the outlaw's reprieve. I hope I was right to fight for his forgiveness. If I was wrong, poor Berta will pay the price. Is it fair? Rose loved an Indian, Cobb cherishes a ghost, even Ross, The Radish, has found his dream girl. Why shouldn't I love who I want? So what if he cannot love me back?

Again, I caress his chest and a thrill shoots through my core. I shouldn't think such scandalous thoughts. Agapito moans, and I sigh. Rose gets up, snaps her journal shut, and leaves without saying anything more.

Today, Agapito almost died at least a dozen times. Maybe he didn't just *almost* die. What if he really did die, but then sprang back to life? Is it a thin line, or an absolute thing? Soon, it will be dark again, and I pray that he will make it through the night.

Monday, September 30

When I awaken, my posterior smarts. How long was I asleep, seated on that blessed barrel, my head resting on the side of Agapito's sickbed? Suddenly, I remember why I've slept sitting up. Fear takes over, and I hasten to assess Agapito's condition.

Is he breathing? What color is his skin? Does he have a pulse? I forget to look in his eyes.

"*¿Viviré?*" His voice sounds scratchy and hoarse.

"Oh, Agapito. Thank goodness. For Heaven's sake. You scared me. I didn't realize that you were awake. What did you say?"

His words trickle forth. "Will I live, *querida*?"

"Well, you'd better live, Agapito. We have to travel today." Gosh, it seems silly of me to say, but the corners of his mouth turn upward. If there's anything a wagon master understands, it is the need to turn the wheels along the trail.

"Where are we?

"We're still somewhere along the Umatilla River. I think we're supposed to spend one more night beside it."

"Oh, I see. It hurts to talk, Dorcas. My head aches, and it is hard to breathe."

I try to console him and he nods when I tell him that he needs to drink some water and eat something. After days of struggling to get anything into him, I'm pleased with how much water he drinks. When breakfast is ready, feeding him is slow but he consumes most of a bowl of mush.

As the hours bump along, the day warms up, and Agapito convinces me to roll the canvas up so he can see outdoors. The sky is blue, benign clouds float slowly by, and the river bends its way between rolling hills. It is beautiful country. Agapito asks me to prop him up. He whispers, "I cannot lie on my back forever."

Though I would prefer to walk alongside, I sit beside Agapito so that he will not have to raise his voice for me to hear him. Finally, he convinces me to let him be alone for a while. Does he need time to himself, or does he figure that I need a change of scenery?

After a couple of hours, plodding along beside the wagon master's prairie schooner as it floats through a sea of gently waving Junegrass, I see what looks like a man sitting on the ground a short distance from the trail. Is he hurt? Did another wagon train leave him behind? Why doesn't he move? Agapito tells me to be careful when I tell him I am going to check on the man.

It only takes a couple of minutes for me to reach him. He doesn't look up when I speak to him, but rather, he sits with his legs extended before him, gazing blankly at a point just beyond his feet.

"Horace. What's wrong? Can I help you?"

Finally, he responds, but he doesn't look at me when he speaks. "This is as far as I'm going."

What about his wife and son? Don't they need him? Do they know he's sitting here like this, not making any sense? "But Horace, we've come so far, and we've almost made it. Maybe you could ride on the wagon for a while." How did the contrary naysayer become my problem?

He looks up slowly, lifts his arm as if it weighed fifty pounds, and points to the west. "Do you see that, lady?"

Is it possible that after five and a half months of traveling together, this man does not know my name? Good Heavens. Impatiently, I respond. "See what?"

Horace sighs and slumps, dejectedly. "You blind? There's a volcano ahead and we're marching straight toward it."

I strain my eyes and peer at the horizon. It seems so far away, but I do see what looks like a solitary mountain in the distance. After blinking several times to moisten my eyes, I'm convinced. "Oh, Horace. That's not a volcano, that's Mount Hood. The fact we can see it means we're practically finished with our voyage."

"Mount Hood is a volcano. It's erupted before, and it will explode again."

"I'm sure there's nothing to worry about, Horace."

"Dig me a grave and lay me down. I can't bear the thought of being roasted to death. Hang me, bury me, and be done with me. I can't live with a volcano. Why didn't anybody tell me there were volcanos here? I can't live in Oregon, I don't have the energy to go back. I'm just too tired. Shoot me now, and get it over with. You know how to use a gun, lady. Put me out of my misery."

"Mr. Blocker. You don't mean that. Lana and Adam are depending on you. How will they get on without you?"

He ignores my mention of his family. "One of these days, that sucker's gonna blow. The top of it is going to blast off into the sky and shoot Hellfire from the depths of Hell. We'll be killed instantly." Horace raises his upper lip in a sneer. "Or, boiling lava will just ooze from the tip of it, slide down the edge, and slowly surround us."

He gasps three times as he inhales, and he sounds as if he might sob. He simpers, "I don't want to be melted."

How many times has Horace predicted that nobody will make it to Oregon? I can't count them.

"What does it matter? We're all going to perish. What's the use?"

I've had enough. "Get your sorry carcass up off of that ground right now."

He lies down on his side rather than obeying me.

"I'm not going to leave you here. Get up this instant."

Horace grunts and rolls over, facing away from me. Does he think that if he can't see me, I'll just go away and leave him here to die?

He doesn't fight me when I drag him from the ground to a standing position. I lead him to the wagon master's wagon and shove him on board.

Dejected, he says, "Fine. I'll die tomorrow when you're not looking. I'll never live to see Oregon, lady."

Tuesday, October 1

Goodness, gracious. I can't believe it is October now, and we're still not *there*. How far must we travel? It's not just Horace Blocker who has had enough. It would be hard to find a single traveler that isn't ready for a long break. If only we didn't have work to do when we get to our destination.

They say that Oregon is just beyond Mount Hood, but we have marched all day. The "volcano" appears to be moving, keeping itself ever beyond our reach. How many times during our journey have we felt like the landmarks remain just beyond us?

Hopefully, today, Horace Blocker is keeping up with his family. He had better stop spouting off about volcanic eruptions. The children have been through so much. The last thing they need is something else to worry about. Maybe it *was* a volcano a long time ago, but now it is just a mountain, and it is in our way. If Mount Hood is our final obstacle, we shall have to overcome it. I'm just relieved that Agapito has so far survived. I no longer fear that he'll expire whenever I turn my back or step away for a minute. He breathes steadily, swallows with ease, and his voice no longer sounds gravelly. It's been half a month since he was shot, and since then, his recovery has been tumultuous.

When the wagons circle at Sand Hollow Creek, I watch Agapito slowly swing his limbs from the bed and then he pushes himself to a standing position with his arms. He steadies himself by holding the rim of the wagon as he shuffles toward the back of the vehicle. How long has it been since he has walked on his own? He's still so weak, but he will get stronger.

I want to encourage him and cheer him on, but worry that I might sound condescending. Without speaking, I help him climb to the ground from the back of the wagon.

He thanks me in Spanish, and says, "I could not do this without you, *querida*."

With a dismissive wave, I reply, "Soon, you'll be back to your old self."

Agapito chuckles. "I do not know about that." It seems like a strange thing for him to say. Horace Blocker, maybe, but not Agapito. Yet, Agapito doesn't sound downtrodden, as Horace always does, despite having survived the outlaw's bullet. Doesn't Agapito want to be his old self? I watch him shuffle along, independently, but he moves like he has aged fifty years. I wonder how rickety he would be if he had to spend another week laid up.

As if summoned by my thoughts, Horace Blocker walks toward Agapito, not fast, but purposefully, which is unusual for Horace. Though I had planned for Agapito to wander on his own, after my visit with Mr. Blocker yesterday, I decide to see what the naysayer has on his mind today.

Agapito stands, steadily, and seems to welcome a conversation.

Horace's jaw shakes as he says, "I had a dream. A terrible nightmare. Only, it was real. It is a warning. We must turn back now while we still can, or we'll all be killed."

I know where this conversation is headed but hold my tongue. I cross my arms cross and bear my weight on one leg. It's a ridiculous fear, but *most* worries *are* irrational. Indeed, there has to be a far greater chance of being devoured by ravenous wolves than to be buried by a mountain full of molten lava. I forgive myself for my own phobias. Then again, how often has disaster struck our expedition? Would I feel differently if Andrew said that he had a premonition? I've grown to accept that my serious son can predict the weather, but his other visions are hard not to explain away as coincidence. Even if there were such a thing as being able to see the future and knowing what will happen before it does, I'm sure that Horace Blocker would not possess such an advanced capability.

As Horace shares his vision of the disaster he imagines with Agapito, I stand, silently, waiting for him to be done. What will Agapito say to the man?

When Horace finally gives Agapito the chance to speak, he points a finger toward the sky. "You are right. That mountain is a dormant volcano. I also have visions, and it will happen exactly as you describe. Only, in my vision, there is a newspaper on the table. Did you see one in your dream? I have seen the date on the heading. Leave a letter, or make a note inside your family Bible. Until the year 2080, we are safe. I do not plan to live that long, do you?"

Horace shakes his head slowly. "No, I'll be lucky to make it through 1850." He looks to the horizon, presumably at the distant peak. "I never expected to make it this far, to be honest."

"You must make me a promise. You will not worry about Mount Hood anymore. You can do this, yes?"

Horace nods, frowns, and turns away. He grumbles, "Who knows?"

As I watch the two men slowly hobble away from one another, I'm amused by Agapito's approach. Surely, he must have made up having had a vision himself. If Horace, the middle-aged prophet of doom, were an average teenaged boy, he would have seen right through Agapito's ruse.

Should I chide Agapito for telling lies or compliment him on his creativity? After years of shepherding greenhorns across the country, the wagon master has learned how to deal with people and their many fears. He was meant to do this work. Leading people to their destiny *must* be Agapito's dream. When he has more fully recovered, I will reassert my intentions to travel with him each year, and live as if we were married, despite the risks of traveling The Oregon Trail, and the heavy toll it exacts. Perhaps many future families will be enticed to sign on with us knowing that a trail-hardened woman is part of the staff.

But first, we must complete *this* journey.

Wednesday, October 2

Sadly, the naysayer's impulses are stronger than the wagon master's assurances.

News spreads from child to child and a wildfire of worry is fueled by an unfortunately timed interview in *The Rolling Home Times*, ensuring that the adults have plenty of trepidation as well. Throughout our long journey, the sensible travelers have ignored most of the defeatist's irrational concerns. Why, now, does everyone believe his dire prediction?

Should I have let the ocean of prairie grass consume the perennial worrywart? If I hadn't rescued the skeptic, our community of travelers wouldn't be so anxious. Though abandoning Horace Blocker makes for a tempting fantasy, I could never have left him to perish on the plains.

When I ask Andrew about interviewing Horace, Andrew says, "He described the eruption of that volcano like he was watching it explode, Mama. It reminded me of the times when I picture things before they happen. I felt guilty for not believing him, until he said that Agapito has had the same vision. Imagine that, two people having exactly the same dream. It's uncanny. What I can't understand is, why haven't *I* felt something? Usually, when something bad is about to happen, I get a ferocious headache. I feel sick to my stomach and have the urge to hork. Anyway, what should we do about the volcano? Should we go somewhere else instead? Should we go way around it instead of passing directly through it?"

"What do you mean, passing directly through it?" For a moment, I ponder Andrew's mention of two people having exactly the same dream and think of those times when Dahlia Jane awakens with night terrors at the exact moment I'm having a frightful nightmare. Thankfully, it doesn't happen as often as it did after our well traveled hen was devoured by a ravenous wolf.

Andrew says, "There's a map in the guidebook. It looks like we go in one side of Mount Hood and out the other."

"It couldn't be. For two thousand miles, we haven't seen a tunnel, and if it weren't for the outlaws, we wouldn't even have seen a cave." For a moment, I recall the interior of the native earth lodge and the eerie, abandoned feeling of being underground.

"Maybe we just skirt the base of it. Should we circle wider than that?"

"I don't think so, Andrew. I don't believe for a moment that there is anything to worry about. The trail is difficult enough. Could you just imagine trying to inch along through a rugged forest on an unblazed trail?"

When we arrive at our evening campsite, a rumble of thunder adds unnecessarily to my fellow emigrants' worries. Horace, the normally slow-moving traveler, bustles about shouting, "Pack up your things. Hitch up the wagons. Sound the trumpet. She's gonna blow." He runs toward Alvah

Nye as if he intends to topple the man. "Hop to it, wagon master. Do your job! Send us back home before you kill us all."

Horace looks to the gathering crowd as if pleading for support. "How many of us must die? Remember Bridget Sawyer? She caught on fire. Then there was Larkin Moon, Carter Wilson, and Ellen Prindle. The cholera got them. Jennie Banyon died of childbed fever. Martin shot himself. Leander was crushed by a wagon. The outlaws killed Clarkson Sawyer, Hannah Knox, and Boss Wheel. Don't forget the witch's Indian and the dirty peddler. Shoot, I've probably forgotten somebody. But *we* survived. For what? Only to be buried in lava? Incinerated? You've heard Captain Meadow's fiery sermons. It's just a matter of time now. Our day of reckoning is here. We gotta go back. We can't travel any farther."

Instead of shuffling about, Agapito strides slowly toward Horace. Rather than seeming fifty years older than his actual age, he only seems thirty years older today. He raises his voice, lifts his arm in the air, and it is almost like he has stepped onto a box. I'm transported, once again, back to the day I first heard his voice on Liberty Street in Independence, Missouri. Confidently and convincingly, he speaks. "A long time ago, there was an evil demon. A powerful sorcerer cast a spell on him, burying him under a massive cone of dirt and rocks, trapping his power and anger beneath the weight. Every three hundred years, the demon's power blows from the top of the mountain. You should worry about that mountain, but not for a long time. The last time it erupted was seventy years ago, according to native historians. That means we shall be safe until the year 2080. How old will you be then? Does anybody plan to live to be two hundred and fifty years old? Do not fear Mount Hood now. Do you understand?"

With a hand on Andrew's shoulder, I mumble, "What do you make of that?" Rather than disown his farcical story, Agapito has made it sound even crazier and shared it with everyone."

Captain Meadows shouts, "Demons and sorcerers. What has become of this expedition? We must place our trust in our Savior, the Lord, God. I've never heard such nonsense. Demons, sorcerers, and volcanoes, *indeed*! You should all be ashamed of yourself. I don't want to hear another word about it."

Agapito says, "If you want to worry about something, how about the weather? The volcano will not erupt for hundreds of years, but the snow will come *this* year. Soon, I fear. We have made it through the Blue Mountains but we still must pass Mount Hood."

Horace screams. "I don't care what you say. We're doomed. Why, we're as good as goners already. This is our last chance to turn back. I'm trying to save you all. Don't you see?" He collapses to his knees and elbows and pounds the ground with his fists. "Why won't you listen to me?"

Horace's fellow travelers turn their backs and walk away. Evidently, Agapito and Captain Meadows have convinced everyone not to worry about Mount Hood, at least for the time being.

Thursday, October 3

During the day we make our way from Well Spring to Willow Creek. We had expected lush flora and plentiful fauna, but the barren land does not provide a glint of Oregon's promised fertile landscapes.

Most of the travelers are low on provisions. As much as possible, we forgo meals to make what little food remains last as long as possible. Whenever opportunity allows, we supplement with foraging, plucking the last of the season's salal berries. They taste like blueberries dragged through a mud puddle, and are leathery as worn out moccasins. It's hard to find juicy berries. What has survived the bears, birds, and first frosts shall have to do, and since we have no alternatives, we pluck them with relish as if they were mana from God in Heaven.

After we set up camp along the creek, men pair up and depart on hunting expeditions. We have many men who fancy themselves able sportsmen. Our scouts have been the most prolific hunters, but lately, big game has been scarce, and small game doesn't stretch far through the hungry rolling village. I watch as Stillman accompanies Dembi Koofai, a rifle in his hand. I've never seen the Shoshone scout hunt with a partner before.

For supper, I set a large pot of water on the fire to boil. As the children bring me cups full of shriveled berries, I make a stew of them. We ran out of flour days ago, but I turn the sacks inside out, releasing trapped meal from the burlap fibers and corners of the bags. When people are hungry, any source of food will do. Most women busily prepare similar broths, including whatever they have without considering what might taste good.

Christopher jogs into camp with a cup of berries for the stew pot. With a worried brow, he says, "Honey and her puppy are hungry. Do we have anything for them?"

He pouts when I apologize. "Did you know that dogs eat berries, Mama? Honey's scrounging for them right along with us. Poor thing."

I express my sympathy, tell him that the dogs will have to make do, and Christopher trots off to refill his cup again.

As I work in camp, I watch Agapito make his rounds, walking slowly from one wagon to the next. Similarly, Cian steps from one campfire to another. He stays for a moment or two and then tramps away as empty handed as when he arrived. When he reaches our camp, he says, "Mind if I warm my hands by your fire for a moment?" Then he tips his head back and says, "My belly grinds fierce, don't you know. Like a miller's gears." He rubs his belly as if trying to comfort himself. "Ran out of camas roots, sorry to say. You wouldn't have a biscuit to share, would you now? I would be forever in your debt." He blinks, expectantly, but I haven't any left or anything with which to make them. If it weren't for the wrecked wagon, I would at least have some of Abigail Trudgeon's withered carrots. I look at Cian, imagine him wriggling his nose like a rabbit, and wonder how long he could make a carrot last.

Dahlia Jane says, "Forget the biscuits, Mama. I want a cake. But we can't have cake. We don't have any eggs. The chickens drowned and we'll never have cake again."

Cian says to the girl, "You must never give up, little one. I'm sure there will be biscuits, chickens, eggs, and cake in Oregon. We should be there in a couple of weeks." The Irish man hungrily licks his lips. "I should like to have a cake as much as you, lass. Well, I must be getting along. Mayhap, Cobb could spare some goat's milk next door."

As sympathetic as I am toward the ever-hungry young man, I hope that Cobb keeps Ridge's milk for the baby rather than giving any away. I suggest, "Why don't you go pick berries? You'll find the children along the creek. Maybe you'll find enough to lubricate the miller's gears!"

"Say, that's a good idea. Why didn't I think of that?"

Horace hobbles into camp as Cian scurries away. He complains, "I'm cold. This place is miserable."

I want to suggest that he will not be cold when the volcano erupts, but I know better. With a little luck, perhaps that topic can be avoided. Instead, I offer, "Why don't you gather some wood and make a fire? Wouldn't Lana and Adam appreciate that?"

Horace grunts. "The boy should fetch wood. Not me."

"Well, where is he?"

"Fishing. Willow Creek. He never is any good to us when there's water to dip a hook into."

"Maybe he'll catch a fish, then. Wouldn't that be welcome?" My mouth waters. I can't help feeling like Cian and imagine myself begging in Horace Blocker's camp for a fat trout. I close my eyes and imagine frying fish and doughy balls of batter in a skillet. Why don't we just butcher one of Cobb's yearling Devons?

Horace gripes, "Doesn't matter if we freeze or starve anyway. We're never going to make it to Oregon. What difference does it make how we perish? Why didn't you just leave me alone in that field? That was a nice place to spend eternity."

"But Horace, think of Lana and Adam. They need you. How are they supposed to get along if something happens to you?"

Horace waves a limp hand and says, "Lana can get another husband. She's still young. Maybe then, she can have that daughter she always wanted. They don't need me anyway. Let Adam fetch firewood. If he could only catch a fish. Then, he could feed the family. He's almost a man now."

As Horace plods away, Rose appears with half a cup of berries, dumps them into the pot and looks blankly about. There's nothing to see, but perhaps she imagines the movement of invisible beings. It hadn't crossed my mind before, but I can't help comparing Horace, Cian, and Rose. She looks at me, frowns, and rolls her eyes. I can't imagine why. I didn't say a word or do anything. As she walks away, I think of all the times when I used to worry about her sanity. Cian is mad with hunger. And Horace is consumed by irrational fears.

Maybe the question isn't whether anybody will make it safely to Oregon, but rather if anyone will maintain their sanity. And yet, who could not be changed by a journey such as this?

It's well past dark and the fire wanes as pairs of hunters return, empty handed. Stillman and Dembi Koofai are the last to return. Stillman says, "We saw plenty of scat, and lots of tracks, but that was it. Nothing moved. We didn't have a chance."

Friday, October 4

There's not much difference between Willow Creek and Rock Creek, except for however many miles there are between them. In this country, there are hundreds of different shades of brown and gray, from beige and tan to sienna and umber. If it weren't for the sky, the whole world would appear drab.

How many Rock Creeks have we passed, anyway? If there were a contest between waterways for the most common moniker, would Rock Creek or Sandy Creek win? It seems there have been too many of both to count. In this case, however, there is no water. Perhaps it babbles delightfully in the spring and early summer, but today, there isn't even a puddle in this barren waterway. We have plenty of water in our barrel, but looking at Rock Creek makes me thirsty just thinking of how dry the riverbed appears.

After teams of hunters set out again in search of meat, I stroll with Agapito along the creek bed as children tumble about searching for berries. Willow Creek, though hardly lush, was more bountiful. My stomach growls as I think of the thin berry soup we'll have tonight compared to the thick black stew we had last night. If this keeps up, we'll be forced to butcher an ox. I banish thoughts of food from my mind.

As we stroll, I realize that we're moving fairly quickly. I say, "It's good to see you getting around so well, Agapito."

"I am getting stronger, no?"

"Yes, Hollis is very pleased, and so am I."

We walk silently for a while. Then I say, "Did you notice that Stillman and Dembi Koofai hunt together?"

Agapito glances at me. We lock eyes. His gaze flickers. It is as if he is looking back and forth, between my left and right eyes, searching for something. "This is new. Does it trouble you?"

Our eyes return to face the stony pathway. As we walk, I step closer to Agapito, and playfully bump my shoulder into his. "I'm not troubled, just nosy. Do you suppose they are friends or is there something *more* between them?"

"I do not know." Agapito is quiet, as if searching his memories for something. He shrugs. "Sometimes, it is hard to tell."

I reach for Agapito's hand and take it into my own. "Yes, sometimes it's hard to tell. Sometimes there's miles of difference between people, and other times, it's a very short trip between friendship and romance, don't you think?"

"You are a wise woman, *querida*." Agapito's head tilts slightly to the side as he glances at me and grips my hand a little bit tighter. "Would you prefer they find love or friendship?"

Why is the world so full of impossible questions? I can't help deflating with a sigh, and say, "Of course, I want Stillman to be happy and find love, but I know it will be a challenge to keep it a secret."

"Sometimes forbidden love is more thrilling. Sharing a secret strengthens a bond."

I squeeze his hand. "Good Heavens. I never thought about it that way, Agapito. But when the thrill of new love wears off, what then? It's sad to think that they would never be accepted anywhere."

Agapito disapprovingly clucks. "Do you think we are getting ahead of ourselves? Perhaps they enjoy hunting together, nothing more."

"The way you speak of forbidden love makes me wonder. Was Merced forbidden, or was there another? Maybe you have known many women."

Agapito chuckles, and it is clear that he understands my question is disguised as a statement. "Merced was my first, last, one and only. At first her family tried to run me off, afraid that I would take her away to Santa Fe. I had to promise we would live in San Antonio for at least five years. They were glad to have Merced at home and married at the same time. When Sarita was born, Merced's mother said it was a dream come true. Five years later, when we told Merced's mother we were moving to Santa Fe, she begged us not to go. Then she tried to convince Merced's father to move the family there as well."

Gently, I nudge, "So, you blame yourself for moving Merced and Sarita to Santa Fe."

He nods. "I blame Santa Fe and I blame myself, but it is not Santa Fe's fault that outlaws attacked our expedition. Still, I have not returned."

When Agapito told me about Merced and Sarita at the campground outside of Independence, I remember him saying that he's never returned to Santa Fe. "Have you been back to San Antonio?"

"Just once. To tell Merced's family. It is the longest trip I have ever made. I will never return. I could not face them again." His chin juts forward, perhaps indicating that nothing could convince him to return there again.

"What about your father and mother? Are they living?"

"Yes, my father is a shopkeeper. I always enjoyed talking with the customers and helping them with their purchases."

"Ah," I say, in a tone that I hope conveys my understanding. "That explains why you are so good with the greenhorns, doesn't it? It's sort of like the customers at your father's shop."

"Hm. I never thought of that. You may be right, *querida*."

Several children pass in front of us, abandoning one berry bush in favor of another. We continue our leisurely stroll, and I ask, "What about your mother?"

With a wistful sigh, he says, "She was the best mother a boy could have. She writes me letters all the time and sends them to Independence. It takes me days to read them." His head tilts down. "I should write to her more often."

Quickly, I add, "And you should visit her too. Couldn't you do that? You wouldn't have to follow the Santa Fe trail to go to Santa Fe, would you?"

A slight frown appears on Agapito's face. "You are right. I can be stubborn, *querida*. Did you know that?"

I chuckle. "It's not your fault. You can't be blamed. You're stubborn because you're a man, but you must go see your mother."

His chuckle matches mine. "Yes. I tell myself that too. But I do not listen very well. It is not my fault. I can not be blamed. I do not listen because I am a man, you see?"

"Very well then, so you understand." After a second, I say, "Tell me more about your mother."

"She loves to make jewelry. Crosses, mostly. Her faith is very important to her."

I step a little closer to Agapito, and reach with my free hand to pat his shoulder. "Your mother sounds sweet. What are your parents' names?"

"My father is called Inocente. My mother is Maria Esperanza."

"I would like to meet them someday, Agapito." I'm glad to see that he looks pleased to hear me say so.

Saturday, October 5

I LOVE THE PRAIRIES, but what I wouldn't give to spend a day in the forest.

After a short day of travel, I'm delighted when we stop at a clear, swiftly moving stream. Just looking at the water is refreshing, yet I can't resist looking around for a secluded place to bathe. I laugh to myself. It might be a good idea to wait until the wagons have finished circling, the oxen are freed from their yokes, and camp has been established. Though it is early afternoon, the air is cold, yet the sun shines brightly. It would have to be a lot colder than this to keep me from taking a dip in the John Day River.

When we've finished settling in, Agapito and I take another walk, leaving the children in camp. As we stroll from camp, he tells me that the river is named for a member of John Jacob Astor's Pacific Fur Company. "They say he went mad after being stripped naked by Indians and left to die. That was not far from here, so they named the river after him. Some forty years ago."

After a short distance to the north, I say, "Where might a lady have a bath around here?"

Agapito holds his arms up, almost shrugging. "What lady?"

My knuckles jab Agapito's arm and I recall Noah's brother, Moses, punching him in that very same spot. Thinking of Noah always makes me feel blue. I look at the man beside me, he smiles, and I realize that I don't care about Noah any longer. Even at the beginning of our trip to Oregon, he still crossed my mind frequently, but I've hardly thought of him in months now. A flutter in my abdomen tells me that it is because of Agapito. I still have many yearnings, but Noah isn't a part of them anymore.

"What lady? Me, of course." I can feel the muscles in my face as it relaxes into a wide grin. "Oh, you're remembering when I used to say that I wasn't very ladylike. You told me not to say that anymore, didn't you?"

"Exactly. I must warn the lady, the water in this stream is painfully cold this time of year."

"I don't care. I've been hankering for a good bath for so long, I'd swim in an ice flow. Don't forget, Agapito. I come from a mountainous town and the river there is made of melted snow. I've practically got ice water in my veins."

"Oh you do, do you? We should have a contest and see who can stay in the water the longest."

"You've got yourself a deal." Suddenly I imagine myself unclothed, and then I imagine disrobing in front of Agapito. Good Heavens, what have I gotten myself into? A thrill shoots through me and warms my cheeks. While tending to Agapito during his infirmity, I've seen more of him than a woman who is not his wife should see. I blink quickly trying to vacate my imagination of him, entirely naked in the broad daylight. I wish I could jump in that river immediately.

"You think you have already won. Am I right?"

I nod and smile. That's *not* what I was thinking at all.

"You must remember, I am a man, therefore, I shall win."

Agapito isn't like most men, assuming himself superior to women. "Just because you're a man, huh?"

"You said it yourself, yes? I am a man, so I am stubborn. That is what it takes to win such a contest."

"Yes, I guess I did say that. How could I forget?" I practically whisper my sordid invitation, only it sounds like an ultimatum. "Then meet me at dark." My heart pounds ferociously in my chest. What are we agreeing to? One week ago, I was afraid for his life. He almost died. Now, only a week later, Heaven help me. I'm just as mad as Horace, Cian, and Rose.

We finish our stroll, and I am so distracted, I have no idea what we're talking about. Does Agapito know that I'm not listening? Hopefully he hasn't been saying anything important.

The afternoon and early evening go by slowly. Rose and Dahlia Jane are camped with Hollis and Charlotte. Andrew and Christopher's blankets are spread beneath the wagon master's awning. I don't know where Stillman is. Perhaps he has night watch. I suppose nobody will notice my absence. It is as if the fates have conspired to allow me to slip away.

There's a sliver of a new moon in the sky. It's about as dark as a night can be. I tiptoe along the dark ribbon of water to the place where we agreed to meet. I listen carefully, for dark nights always rekindle my fear of wolves. Tonight, they're quiet, so quiet that I can hear the thumping of my heart—or am I imagining it?

"Dorcas!"

I gasp and jump. It's as if I'm startled, and yet I expected Agapito to be here.

He says, "I did not know if you would come."

"You didn't?"

"I thought you would, but I was not certain."

"Ooh." Though I've been anxious all afternoon and evening, I never once considered *not* showing up. My only question was how to slip away unnoticed. All I can think to say is, "How *are* you, Agapito?"

"Mad as a cranky old trapper."

I can't help laughing. "John Day. I see. Are you sure you have recovered enough for...." It takes a long time for Agapito to answer. Still, I leave my question unfinished.

"One can never be completely sure of anything, *querida*. If you are willing, I will take my chances. What about you, Dorcas? Are you sure?"

"I told you, I have ice water in my veins." I'm lying to him. It's as if hot molten lava pumps from my heart with every quick beat. I should demurely turn away, but instead, I remove my dress slowly. Agapito does not turn away either. Then, I slowly unbutton the shirt I wear beneath my dress and try not to think of the man it once belonged to.

Agapito slowly unbuttons his shirt and lifts his head as he gulps. I release the strap between my breasts, the one that forces the suspenders together, and unbutton them from Larkin's trousers as Agapito's shirt falls to the ground. There's a nervous sound to his laughter as he says, "I thought this was a race, *querida*."

I shiver as a cool breeze reminds me that it is October. "It is not a race, Agapito. It is an endurance contest, isn't it?" I quickly unfasten the buttons on my trousers, kick them aside, and spread my legs slightly. I take a deep breath, place my hands on my hips, and remember how I felt on Independence Rock, months ago. "If it's a race, I'm winning." Goodness gracious. What has gotten into me? I can't believe I'm doing this.

It's dark, but my eyes have adjusted. Maybe he can see me as well as I can see him, but I don't care anymore.

He says, "*Muy bonita*, so lovely." His fingers release the buttons on his trousers, then he steps away from them and says, "*Diosa de la luna*, my moon goddess." All he's wearing now is a small bandage that covers what remains of his wound. I could stare at him all night. Instead, he steps forward. Our lips join briefly, he takes my hand, and we step into the water. It doesn't matter how cold it is, I'm already numb.

We make our way to the deepest point and the water reaches chest level. I spread my legs and curl my toes around smooth river rocks to maintain my balance in the swift river current. Agapito stands before me, wraps his arms around me, and pulls our bodies close together. He whispers over the sound of rushing water, "Just because we are frozen does not mean we have to be cold."

Less than a week ago, I thought Agapito looked as frail as an eighty-year-old man. How quickly things can change. His hands explore my back, and he kisses me fervently. As his hands travel from my shoulder blades to the small of my back, I can't help but wonder, what he will do with his hands next? Suddenly, we freeze.

I whisper. "Did you hear that?"

Agapito says, "I wish that I did not."

A man's voice repeats. "Who's there?"

In Agapito's ear, I say, "I'd better go."

Agapito shouts, telling the man his name and to wait a minute.

I splash my way to the river bank and find a tree to hide behind while dressing.

Agapito yells again. "I told you my name. Now, who are you?"

Dembi Koofai steps forward. "It is me." A deer is draped over the scout's shoulders, and Stillman is beside him. "We have meat. Stillman shot a deer."

Sunday, October 6

While dozing off to sleep last night, I wondered what we might say in the light of day. Last night, we behaved like impetuous young lovers, or would-be lovers. I think of Agapito's demeanor. Will he act as if nothing happened? Perhaps he will shy away from me, ashamed, as if he had violated Merced's trust. Maybe in the light of day, he'll think I looked better in the dark. Not once has he mentioned my proposal to travel back and forth between Missouri and Oregon as his woman, not his wife. How long has it been since I told him my plan?

In the morning, my mind is still spinning through the possibilities. The scouts quickly deliver generous portions of Stillman's deer to each wagon. It won't last long, but we may as well enjoy it while we can.

Agapito is usually up early, but this morning, he is the last to rise. He rubs his eyes and says, "Something smells good!"

Dahlia Jane shouts, "It's breakfast, silly."

"Oh. Nice to have breakfast, *amorcita*."

I'm seated beside the campfire. I ask, "Will you have some?"

He says, "How could I resist?" He wishes everybody a good morning on the way to my side. Then he squats beside me and says, in a low voice that only I can hear, "I win."

"What do you mean?"

He whispers, "I stayed in the river longer than you did. I win. Only I did *not* win the prize I hoped for. You left too soon."

I glance around. Stillman and Dembi Koofai are gone, but Andrew, Christopher, and Rose lay about, enjoying a day off and evidently pleased to have full bellies for a change. In a low voice I say, "Thanks to your scout. If it weren't for him, I am sure I would have won. In fact, I might still be there, frozen like a statue."

"Thanks to your adopted son. If he had not shot that deer, there is no telling what might have happened."

I take a breath, intending to say that we should talk about that, but raised voices at The Hub distract our conversation. I say, "Oh, no. Not again." I look into Agapito's dark brown eyes and say, "It's Bobby and Wayne."

The children follow as Agapito and I step urgently toward the center of the circled wagons. The crowd grows quickly as travelers hotfoot it across all of the imaginary spokes of our invisible wheel. It may be Sunday, a day of rest, but that won't stop Bobby and Wayne if something's going to spark their tempers.

With my hands on my hips, I say, "What's the cause of this ruckus?"

They turn toward me as one and point.

"I didn't do anything."

Bobby says, "Not you. Her."

Dahlia Jane wraps her arms around my leg and clamps on tightly.

"My daughter?"

Wayne says, "Yes. She's been walking around asking everybody where they're going to live. Nobody can answer."

"Then why are you fighting?"

Bobby answers. "Wayne says he wants to go where you go."

"But you don't want to?"

Bobby shakes his head. "Me and Serena also want to go where you go, but Wayne says you won't have us."

"So you're fighting about what I might or might not say? But you agree you want to live where I homestead?"

"I know. Ain't that dumb?"

"Wait, do you mean ain't that dumb to fight about, or ain't that dumb to want to go where I go?" I look around and everybody looks confused. To the crowd, I say, "Does anybody know where they want to go when we get to Oregon?"

Miranda says, "These knuckleheads never planned beyond getting to Oregon. I plan to set up shop in Oregon City. Sully Pierce and I are going to be married, and we'll run the store that Hannah always dreamed of."

Our oldest traveler, Minor Shaw says, "We're going to find a place in Oregon City too."

Captain Meadows says, "We didn't come all this way to live in some crowded city. We came for free land. Fertile land. Remember what they say, the land of milk and honey. That's what we're here for."

Fritz Franzwa, who doesn't speak much, says, "Would you like to see a map? I just happened to be looking at one this morning after breakfast."

The guidebooks show how to get there, but Fritz's map, rough as it is, shows the place's features. It would have been great to see this ages ago. "Have you had this all along, Fritz? Why didn't you show us sooner?"

He shrugs. "Nobody asked me."

Captain Meadows says, "What are our options, Fritz? Where do people go? What looks best to you?"

Fritz holds the map facing away from him, and says, "There's the Willamette River, Champoeg Creek, Pudding River, Molalla River, and the Clackamas River. Depends on what land isn't already taken."

Captain Meadows points to the map and says, "I'd like to build a town along that one there, the Molalla River."

The other members of The Committee, the Crouses and Lathams, say they'll follow Captain Meadows, and Travis Latham suggests they name the town Mortimer. Mortimer, Oregon. It doesn't sound appealing to me, but Esther Bump says she'd like to homestead there and Addie Bull quickly agrees. Why don't I feel sad to know that they'll reside somewhere I won't? If anything, I'll miss Luella Meadows, the Captain's wife, more than the friends I set out with a year ago.

Galusha says, "I want to live near Pudding River." It comes as no surprise to hear that the Grosvenors, Blockers and Reids plan to follow Galusha to the promised land of pudding.

Fritz says, "I reckon to try that one, Champoeg Creek, but I don't know why." The Franklin and Bellows families agree with Fritz, and everyone else is disappointed to hear that the blacksmith, Schuyler Steele, intends to settle there also.

Dahlia Jane says to me, "Where are we going, Mama?"

I shrug. Then I point to the one that looks closest to Mount Hood. "How about that one?"

Fritz says, "The Clackamas River?"

I nod and Agapito whispers from nearby, "Good choice."

Fritz says, "Well, we don't have to decide now. Maybe there are other choices. Oregon is growing fast and I don't know how old this map is. I aim to make a new one."

Travis asks Galusha what he plans to call his town.

Samuel Grosvenor answers for him. "If you can have Mortimer, Oregon, why then, we'll call ours Galusha. Galusha, Oregon. Don't that have a ring to it?"

Landon Young says, "We're headed for the Willamette River. That's the biggest one, I think. We'll name the place later, or join a place that's already started. I expect my sister, Sarah Terwilliger, and her kids will join us." The Carpenters, Weavers, and Grimes family crowd around Landon, clamoring to join the Youngs and Terwilligers.

Galusha says, "What about the rest of you?" It's as if he thinks whoever has the most fellows wins.

Berta wraps her arm around Ross's waist and says, "Ve go vith her." I'm pleased.

Hollis says, "I think we'd like to go with Dorcas Moon, also." I'm so glad our new friends will be joining us.

Cobb says, "Me too." I would have been surprised if the Banyons didn't join us. We've grown so close as travel neighbors.

Bobby says, "So what's it going to be, ma'am? You going to let us join you?"

"Why not?" The hot heads have grown on me. They're mostly harmless. They're really only trouble to one another. Perhaps they'll elect me sheriff.

On the way back to camp, I think about our fracturing village. Almost everybody stated their plans. I take inventory in my head and realize that nobody asked Stillman, and he didn't say. Alvah Nye was silent also. I suppose it's assumed that Agapito, Arikta, and Dembi Koofai will return to Independence and guide a new batch of greenhorns to Oregon next year. What will the Banyons, Letts, Bonds, and Hortons do when they find out I plan to join the wagon master's crew?

I didn't realize that Agapito was still at my side. He says, "This usually happens earlier. I am surprised it took this long, *querida*."

Soon it will be time for everyone to say goodbye. I don't much like goodbyes. I say, "I am not sure I want to live in a fertile, settled valley. I didn't come all this way to be the same woman I was before."

Agapito asks, "If you could make a town called Dorcas, where would it be? Of all the places we have been, where would you put it?"

"Near Fort Bridger, I suppose."

"That is good country."

Does that mean that he would settle there with me? Has he forgotten what I told him about joining him along the trail again next year?

Monday, October 7

Andrew says we marched seventeen miles today. We find ourselves along another remnant of a waterway at a place called China Hollow. Agapito tells us that tomorrow we'll reach the mighty Columbia River, and then, the final leg of our journey will begin. How many times have we felt that we were beginning the last segment of the trail, only to find out that many more obstacles remain?

After supper, Agapito and I stroll a short distance from camp. The scouts have found some grass for the stock. It's sparse, but it's the best we've found in days. The nearer we get to our destination, the more uncertain I am that it will meet expectations.

Agapito says, "We have never before traveled with a herd this big."

The outlaw's well-fed stock makes the gaunt creatures that began the journey with us, nearly two thousand miles back, seem all the more impoverished. The ribs of most of the cattle are visible, and many of the horses are so boney, it's hard to guess how much weight they've lost. I frown at Agapito and say, "I wish we could let them graze for a couple of weeks. Just looking at them makes me hungry." Stillman's deer didn't last for long.

I'm not sure whether the animals or people are more malnourished. If it weren't for our clothing, I'm sure our bones would appear with prominence, barely covered by our skin.

Agapito stops walking and looks at me. "We must get to the other side of Mount Hood. Then, they will fatten up fast."

As we wander indiscriminately among the stock, the cattle ignore us. I can't resist stroking their necks, despite their ambivalence. When we began our voyage, we were told that the Devons would fare well. They're emaciated now, but they have held up, as well as, if not better than, the other breeds of cattle. It makes me sad to think of Scrapple, and our team of oxen, swept away by the Grande Ronde River, little more than two weeks ago. And poor Hardtack. If any creature deserved to take it easy on sweet and plentiful meadows in Oregon, it was our lead oxen.

Agapito laughs as Muddy George's sole surviving donkey muzzles his pocket, as if searching for a treat. An image of the affable oaf's wide, ear to ear grin appears in my mind and I try to resist picturing him as he died, staked to the prairie. The little gray donkey must miss the man and whatever he carried in his pockets. I often think of George when I run the tips of my fingers across the teeth of the mane comb in my pocket.

Nearby, Henry Trudgeon's mule shakes its head from side to side. Its ears flop comically and the critter coughs. Perhaps the mule's lungs are bothered by the cloud of dust that its movement tossed into the air. I say, "I wonder what Henry called this mule."

Agapito says, "Is this the one that can smell the gold?"

Until Agapito answered, I hadn't realized that I had spoken my thoughts. "Let's call her Motherlode. What a ridiculous notion. If it hadn't been for this mule, maybe Henry would have given up looking for gold. Maybe he would have abandoned the idea of spending another summer prospecting. Poor Abigail is probably still waiting for Henry's return. Imagine, never knowing what became of her husband. Rose thinks Henry's ghost sits on the porch with her." I can't contain or prevent a loud harrumph. "Imagine that."

Agapito changes the subject. "What do you plan to do with your share of the money?"

I guess he doesn't want to talk about ghosts, or maybe it's gold-sniffing mules that he'd rather not discuss. I say, "From selling the outlaw's herd?"

"Yes, *querida*."

"I should save the money, but I'd like to buy this cremello." Before I know it, the mane comb, which goes everywhere with me, appears in my hand. "Do you remember the day that Larry Pritchard passed through camp?"

"What a sad story he told."

"I hope he made it home to Missouri." What if I were Larry's mother? I wish I could not imagine her heartbreak. "Remember, Larry said his brother's horse was called, Señorita?"

"I do."

"If possible, I'd like to purchase Señorita, Motherlode, and that dopey little donkey."

Gwibunzi nickers and nudges Señorita aside. Agapito strokes the mustang's withers and admires the exotic mare. "This one reminds me of you, Dorcas."

"That's funny. I never told anyone this, but I feel the same way. If I were a horse, I would want to be Gwibunzi."

As if it were a serious topic, Agapito says, "Before or after she was captured?"

What a stupid question. I can't help laughing, and Agapito explodes with laughter also.

He doesn't hear the clumping beat of hooves behind him. Rio trots up to him and nudges his backside, tossing him off balance. "Ay, yi, yi, Rio is a jealous one, no?" He turns toward his mare, and says, "I have missed you, *mi caballo dulce.*" I repeat the Spanish phrase, and he clarifies: "My sweet horse."

I hand Agapito the mane comb as he coos into her ear. Standing with this man among the horses makes me almost as happy as being with him in the river. I say, "I don't care about money, mansions, or earthly possessions, but whenever I come across a beautiful horse, I just want to keep it all to myself. They make me selfish and greedy, I suppose. They're sort of like men—no two are the same. Each is a one-of-a-kind, just gotta steer clear of the dunderheads."

"Ahh, I see. But I am not a dunderhead. If I were a horse, which one would I be?"

I glance at my Andalusian stallion, Blizzard. How long has it been since I've had a chance to ride him? Gwibunzi tosses her head about and trots away. I say, "A handsome man catches my eye, but the sight of a beautiful horse, running, makes me feel wild and free." I place my hands on Agapito's shoulders and say, "I'm sorry. You're not a horse. If you were a four legged animal," my eyes blink rapidly, and then I continue, "you would be an antelope." His brown eyes widen and I can see my reflection in them. "Oh, listen to me, I guess I've become as loco as all the other greenhorns."

"No. It is not crazy, Dorcas. I like it. I like it very much."

Tuesday, October 8

It's the middle of the night. I don't want to get up, but it is my turn to stand watch. I'd rather take the first half of the night than have the graveyard shift, but I insist on doing our share, which means standing guard. Tonight, my partner is Stillman.

Waking Stillman isn't usually a challenge. After traveling all day, yesterday, Stillman and Dembi Koofai set out in pursuit of game, again. They returned to camp well after dark, with nothing to show for their troubles. If Stillman got two hours of sleep, then he must have fallen asleep at once. What if I just let him sleep? I could watch over the camp and our herd by myself. It's against Boss Wheel's rules, but we don't follow all of his rules anymore. What if something happened? I would never forgive myself and Stillman would be blamed. I couldn't stand that.

It's hard to make out his words through the gravelly sound of his voice as he sits up. "Hold your horses. I'm coming." He shakes and looks like he's in pain as he stretches his face in a long yawn. "Oh, it's you, Dorcas."

Normally, I would have shaken him and let him rise on his own, but I know that when one is short on sleep, the temptation to roll over and return to slumber is great.

"We have watch tonight, remember?"

He grumbles as he rises from his place beneath the wagon and quickly stows his blankets. "How could I forget?"

I pour a thick cup of cold coffee, left over from last night, and hand it to him. "I promise it's gonna taste terrible, but it might help you stay awake."

Even in the dark of night I can see his upper lip curl. It is as if he's tasted the offensive brew before putting the cup to his lips.

As if it were medicine and I were a doctor, I say, "Drink up, and let's go." We make our way to relieve the first guard.

The new moon is fully blocked by ominous, low hanging clouds. I don't remember it being so chilly when I went to bed last night. Perhaps a cold front has descended from the north. I shiver, wish that I had something more to wear, and bemoan the loss of my coat when our schooner sank in the Grande Ronde.

We stand between the herd and the wagons, shoulders perpendicular, and heads turned away from one another. Stillman watches over camp. My protective gaze is focused on the stock.

I say, "You and Dembi Koofai are spending a lot of time together." As soon as my words are spoken, I wish that I had found another way to say them. I try not to sound motherly when I talk to Stillman.

It takes a long moment before he responds. "Yeah."

"That's nice." I stretch the word nice in a way that I hope encourages Stillman to say more.

"I asked him to teach me how to track and hunt better. He's an expert. But he doesn't talk much. He points, makes gestures, and grunts a lot."

"I see."

"I don't mind, though. At first it felt awkward, spending so much time together and not saying anything, but now, I realize how unnecessary spoken words are."

"Have you developed a *special* friendship?"

He repeats my words back to me. "A special friendship?" When he says it a second time, he sounds irritated. "Oh, a *special* friendship." He huffs and sounds agitated. "I don't know. I wish I knew and at the same time, I don't want to find out. I'm just happy to spend time with him. Special friendship!" He huffs again, "I don't want to talk about *that*, Dorcas." He whispers, "Why do you always want to bring that up?"

"I'm sorry. I don't mean to pry." But it's a lie. Why else would I ask? I'm always curious about people's romances when they're clandestine, but then, when they are plain for everyone to see, I turn envious. In Stillman's case, I just want him to be happy. I know it won't be easy for him.

He says, "I'll make a trip around the stock."

When he's gone, my body relaxes. Why am I so tense? There's something off-putting about talking to someone with your backs to each other. I know it makes Stillman uncomfortable when I'm nosy. Now, I wonder. What's with that elusive guide? Not so long ago, I jumped to the conclusion that Dembi Koofai and Rose were courting. Is Dembi Koofai interested in Stillman? It's clear to me how Stillman feels, but what about the scout? My instincts have been wrong before. I feel compelled to speak with Dembi Koofai, yet this is none of my business. Stillman will never forgive me if I intervene. It's hard to deny the urge to be helpful, even when such assistance is not welcome.

When Stillman returns, he tells me that he can't see a thing. Now it's my turn.

When it begins to snow as I make my first trip around the perimeter of our encampment, I know that I should be horrified. A blizzard would be a disaster. How would we get the wagons over Mount Hood and the Cascade Mountains?

Instead, I'm jubilant. If I've been homesick for anything, it's tall mountains and fluffy snow. Last winter, we barely saw flurries when we wintered in Missouri. It was a welcome break from what seemed like a lifetime of winter.

It's a good thing that it is dark and I'm practically alone. I twirl like a pixie, tip my head back, and catch snowflakes on my tongue. Sometimes adults need moments when they can forget about their obligations and act like children again.

By morning, there's six inches of snow. When morning dawns, sparkling white rather than brown and gray, I am elated.

Galusha Gains is in a foot-stomping fury. Samuel Grosvenor reminds us that he tried to warn everyone. They look at me accusingly, as if part of the job of the night watchman is to prevent snowfall. When Horace Blocker sits on his fanny in the snow and refuses to take a single step, I don't get involved. Let somebody else set the man straight today.

I walk ahead of the wagons, following the trail that somehow remains visible even beneath half a foot of precipitation. I feel powerful, as if I were the creator and invented winter.

Wednesday, October 9

Yesterday, after a grueling day of marching through slushy, melting snow in a deep canyon, we reached the Columbia River at Biggs Junction. I just looked at it and went to bed.

This morning, I feel the same way that I did yesterday. I tell myself, "It's the mighty Columbia. We've done it. We've finally done it." After months of laboring to get here and so much loss of life, we have reached Oregon at last. We should be rejoicing, yet I can't muster an ounce of enthusiasm.

As we trudge along the plateau, I can't help sneering at the disappointing waterway. What good is a river that cannot nurture the surrounding countryside? The land of milk and honey, indeed.

Charlotte walks beside me. We haven't conversed much. It seems that neither of us has much to say, although normally, our conversations come easily.

My stomach growls. This morning's shrivel berry soup did not provide much nourishment.

Charlotte looks at me and frowns. "I can't remember being this hungry. We've always been fortunate. I don't know how much farther we can go without something to eat."

I grit my teeth. Charlotte is right. We must have food. How is it possible that there is nothing to eat? After months of listening to the hunters in our party brag about their prowess and insult each others' skills, why are we without meat? One of the reasons we signed on with this outfit was the prospect that our native scouts would provide food for us. I close my eyes and remember the small deer that Stillman shot a few days ago. We've had nothing since. Instead of complaining out loud, I mumble sympathetically to Charlotte. But I don't even know what I just said.

At mid-morning, we reach the swift moving Deschutes River, which empties into the Columbia. I feel dizzy, rub my forehead and wish for a moment to sit and rest. The wagons slow and I step forward several paces. There are a dozen Indians at the edge of the river. It appears that they operate a transport service. They aren't dressed like the native people we met on the prairies. Instead, they wear clothing that looks more like what we wear. I watch as our men approach the Indians.

The rickety looking transport doesn't inspire much confidence. I try to concentrate. Where have I seen similar operations? I think back to our first couple of river crossings, and remember what looked like a raft perched on top of two canoes. This river isn't nearly as wide as the Kaw, but it looks treacherous, nevertheless.

Glancing back at the men, I notice their posture, leaning toward the Indians as their animated arms gesture rapidly. The Indians, on the other hand, stand with arms crossed over their chests or hands on their hips. I don't need to hear them to understand that the Indians are saying, "That's our price, take it or leave it." How bad could it be? Surely, we could afford to pay a dollar or two per wagon. Then, I recall the fact that we're broke. Our funds had been running low when we lost the wagon and everything in it, including the last several dollars of our family's meager savings. I fumble the mane comb in the pocket of my loose fitting trousers. My family should be paying their fair share to get across the river. It's bad enough that we must use Alvah Nye's wagon. We can't even contribute to its operation. He says that we're doing him a favor by driving it for him while he leads the wagon train, but we should at least pay the toll.

At the fringe of the negotiations, Galusha steps toward an Indian and shoves his palms into the man's chest. The ferryman stumbles and falls to the ground, then springs back to his feet brandishing a Bowie knife. His hand moved so swiftly, I didn't see him pull the dagger from a sheath tied to his leg.

Wayne and Bobby jump forward and grab Galusha by the elbows, tugging him away from the Indian who taunts Galusha in a language he does not understand. Alvah speaks to the angry man and convinces him to put the knife away. "Forgive us. This man sometimes forgets to mind his manners."

Nearby, Agapito stands with an Indian who appears to be in charge of the ferry service. Agapito says, "The price was four dollars per wagon until Galusha Gains elected himself chief negotiator. Now, the price is five dollars. Who will be the first to cross?"

The wagons line up and prepare to take their turns at the crossing. I make my way to Agapito's side and say, "We can't afford to cross. We don't have any money left."

Agapito says, "Do not worry, *querida*. Alvah has paid for the transport of his wagon and the master's."

My hand covers my mouth.

Agapito nods. "Yes, if it were not for Alvah's savings, we could not pay to transport the master's wagon. You remember, Boss Wheel carried the money himself."

It takes a couple of hours before the last wagon is deposited on the western shore of the Deschutes River. The trail leads away from the crossing up a steep, rocky incline. An hour later when we reach the top of the hill, I want to collapse in a heap, tired and hungry as I am. Mercifully, we stop for our mid-day meal. There may not be anything to eat, but the opportunity to rest is welcome.

I'm stunned when Arikta sets a crate on the ground and lifts a heavy salmon from it. He hands me the fish and says, "For your dinner." He smiles, lifts the box from the ground and steps toward Cobb's wagon.

I look at the fish and wonder how I will fit it into the skillet. My mouth waters so hard, my jaw hurts. I've never appreciated the gift of a meal more.

After the fish is gone and the skillet is stowed, I step a few feet from the wagon. From the hill's summit, I can see far into the distance.

Agapito appears beside me. "Have you ever seen anything like this, *querida*?"

I shake my head in wonder.

He points to the south. "That is Mount Jefferson. There is Mount Hood. To the north you see Mount Adams, and look beyond. Can you see it? That is Mount St. Helens. The Indians call it the Smoking Mountain."

"I thought Horace had gone mad. Maybe he is right to worry. Look at all those volcanoes."

At the end of the day, we reach The Dalles. This waypoint at a bend in the Columbia River forces emigrants to make a hard choice.

Friends and foes argue mightily. Galusha argues to ride the rafts from The Dalles to our destination, and Captain Meadows insists that we follow The Barlow Road to the south of Mount Hood. Agapito tells the men about the dangers, highlighting the pros and cons of each. Neither sounds like a good plan, but what choice do we have?

Despite all of the bad things that can happen, one way or the other, the fact that Boss Wheel preferred The Barlow Road convinces many, myself included. Alvah reminds the travelers that many who take the waterway drown before reaching Oregon City. Ultimately, Captain Meadows polls the men, and a slight majority prefer the road.

Galusha furiously stomps. "You'll be sorry." He threatens to leave us and ride the river anyway.

As Galusha and his sidekick storm off in anger, I wonder, what if he does? Wouldn't that be marvelous?

Thursday, October 10

I haven't spent much time in the wagon that Alvah Nye gave us after we lost our prairie schooner in the Grande Ronde River disaster. Most of my nights have been spent beside Agapito in the wagon master's rig, but he's much improved. He sleeps through the night, can get on and off the wagon without assistance, and has returned to most of his usual activities. I must admit that nights are more restful now that I can recline while sleeping. It took a couple of nights to get used to sharing the wagon with a hunting dog and her growing puppy.

It surprises me that Alvah's wagon is so heavily laden. The front third of his wagon has an enormous heap of something under thick blankets, tightly tied beneath thick rope. It would be nice to stretch out while sleeping, but it isn't possible to fully extend in Alvah's overcrowded wagon. Maybe the tall man didn't mind sleeping curled up in a ball. Who am I to complain? Not having a wagon of our own, I should be glad to have a covered place to sleep at night.

My curiosity always gets the better of me. I would like to peek beneath the coverings and see what the young man carries with him. Instead, I run my hands over the cargo and try to guess what it is. I ask Christopher, who knows Alvah best, what Alvah carries in the back of his wagon.

"I don't know, Mama. I don't remember seeing all of that at the beginning of the trip. Maybe he picked up something along the way." Christopher shrugs. It's clear that he doesn't care. Whatever it is, it's solid, maybe iron or steel, and rectangular shaped. I shall have to work around it and put it out of my mind.

With my knees bent and my back on the firm bed board, I look up into the wagon bonnet. Christopher sits on the floor with Honey's puppy. I should be bustling about, doing chores, or seeing if anybody needs help with anything, but all I want to do is rest. I say, "Have you found a name yet?"

Christopher speaks quickly. "For the puppy? I don't know. I've been thinking of calling him Boss. After Boss Wheel. What do you think of that, Mama?"

"That's a nice tribute, Christopher." What do I think of that? Naming a dog *Boss*. I imagine calling the dog for dinner and start to laugh.

"What's so funny, Mama?"

"Think of it, honey. Here, Boss. Sit, Boss. Doesn't that seem amusing? Who wouldn't want to tell a boss what to do? And imagine telling Boss Wheel, in particular."

Christopher laughs along with me. As his laughter wanes, he says, "Didn't you like Boss Wheel, Mama?"

With a sigh, I admit that at first, I thought the man had way too many rules. "As time went on, the man grew on me. I think he grew to appreciate us, too. I'll never forget the time he said, 'You'll do.' That was the first night I stood watch."

"I remember. That was the night some Indians tried to make off with the horses."

"That's right."

"Were you scared?"

"You better believe it. Remember how I screamed?"

"I do. I thought that was so we would hear you and come and help."

"Well, that's what I like to think also." I also remember the time I was chased by Indians back to the wagons. What might have happened if they had caught up to me before I made it back to the wagons. Would Boss Wheel or Agapito and the scouts have come to my rescue? Maybe it's better not to think of it.

Christopher says, "Another week, and Boss will have to be weaned. That's what Alvah says. What does that mean, Mama?"

I tell him that the puppy will need to eat on his own rather than getting his meals from his mother. "Boss will need to spend more time away from Honey."

"Gosh, Mama. That's going to be hard."

"Really? I think Boss spends more time with you than with his mother. Maybe it won't be as hard as you think."

Christopher tells me that he's been working on Boss's training. "Do you think Boss will be a good hunter, like Honey is?"

"I'm sure she will be. Maybe Alvah can help you with Boss's training."

"Aw, he's too busy now. Ever since he took over the wagon train, he never has time for hunting or the dogs." Christopher doesn't say it, but he sounds resentful. It's as if he's sore at the man for not spending enough time with him rather than the dogs, and I remember how out of sorts Christopher felt when Lucky dominated Alvah's time. Christopher concludes, "I wish Boss Wheel was still alive. If he were running the wagon train, Alvah could go hunting more. We wouldn't be hungry then, would we, Mama?"

"No, I guess not. I never met a better hunter than Alvah, did you, Christopher?"

"No. Galusha Gains claims he's the best hunter, but I don't know. I guess he's brought in some meat, but not as much as Alvah, Arikta, and Dembi Koofai."

After a minute, Christopher asks me if I'd like to pet the puppy. Though I'd rather not, I know I need to get used to the animal living with us. I run my fingers through the dog's soft fur and it tries to nibble on my finger with its sharp teeth.

"He doesn't mean to hurt you, Mama. Alvah says that's how dogs explore the world. With their noses and mouths." He puts Boss back on the floor of the wagon, and then says, "What do you think about Boss Wheel's fortune, Mama? Where do you think it is? Everybody's talking about it, everywhere I go. You don't think it got left behind in the cave, do you?"

I replay being held against my will in the outlaw's cave. I blink at the memory of The Viper shooting Boss Wheel. For the life of me, I can't remember what happened to Boss Wheel's coins and banknotes.

Christopher repeats. "Do you?"

"No, son. I keep trying, but I just can't remember if it was still there or not. I was too worried about Agapito."

Friday, October 11

After making camp at Tygh Creek, I consider saddling Blizzard or Gwibunzi and riding off alone for a while. Instead, I walk to the east in search of firewood. It's more plentiful in this valley than many other places we've been, yet still, I venture from camp.

After walking about fifteen minutes, I'm surprised to see a young man in ripped clothes, with no hat. His sand colored hair is messy and his skin looks sunburned. He doesn't seem to notice me. I don't want to scare him, so I call to him quietly before shouting louder and louder.

The man walks like he's in a trance, and I wonder if this is what it is like for Rose. But surely, the man isn't a ghost. Why doesn't he hear me?

I make my way toward the stranger. When I'm standing in front of him, he stops, stands, and blinks quickly, as if trying to dry his eyes so he can make sense of what he sees. Then he opens his mouth and stutters. "Who... who. Ooh." He takes a breath as if speaking exhausts him. "Who are you? Where did you come from?" Tears drip from the corners of his eyes. I've never seen anybody look more grateful than this man. "Are you an angel?"

I say, "Hi, Mister. I'm Dorcas, and no, I'm no angel."

"Where are we?"

"This is Tygh Valley. What's your name and where are you headed?"

"Oh. Or... Oregon. We're going to Oregon." He frowns and flinches. "But I'm the only one left." He hangs his head. "Oh, dear." Now his tears look like they're made of sorrow rather than gratitude. Stuttering again, he says, "I am Linc. Lincoln Collie, from Illinois."

I tell the young man that he must join us and he obediently follows.

On the way to camp, he says, "Good thing you found me. I don't know how much farther I could have gone."

As I build up our camp fire, I say, "I wish I could feed you. We don't have much, just a little bit of stock. It's thin, but you're welcome to share it with us." It would be generous to call the soup thin. It's barely more than fish flavored water, the last of what remains from the salmon Arikta passed out at the Deschutes River.

Distracted, Linc shakes his head slowly, and his torso shifts from side to side as he mutters ominously, "Twenty-five wagons. All of them, gone. Nobody made it. Nobody but me. Even my wife and child...." Linc chokes as he inhales, coughs, and then sobs. He sniffles and rubs dirt onto his face. "Dead. I couldn't even bury them." His head droops, and he presses his palms into his temples. "I just left them there. I took a few steps away and meant to go back. Only, I kept walking. I didn't mean to, but I just left them there—where they died. God help me. How could I have done such a thing?"

Agapito says, "You must not blame yourself, Mr. Collie. Who was your wagon master?" It would seem Agapito holds the leader of the expedition to blame, not young Linc.

Linc turns his head, looks at Agapito, and then glances at the rest of the people gathered about the campfire before turning back to face me. "Mr. Delano. Mr. Gregory Delano, also from Illinois. Only, he's not a wagon master. He had a guide book, read a newspaper article, and talked to a man in Missouri about the Oregon Trail. That man told him about the *secret* passageway from the Malheur River to Oregon."

I think back to that day we considered taking the cutoff in hopes of avoiding the outlaws. What if we had followed the Malheur River? Would we have avoided the run-in with The Viper, Sloan, and The Radish? Maybe, Boss Wheel, Hannah Knox, and Clarkson Sawyer would still be alive. Agapito wouldn't have been shot. Instead, we would have suffered the same fate as Captain Delano's wagon train. We'd be lucky if anybody survived. If my memory serves me, I believe Galusha Gains made a case for taking the cutoff, and I was almost convinced that we should follow him instead of Captain Meadows.

Everyone listens in horror as Linc goes on to say, "Watching everybody die was bad enough. But ooh, it was torture watching them suffer. First, we ran out of food. We rationed our water, barely touching our tongues to it when we needed a drink. The sun cooked us and made our thirst even worse. We kept walking west, hoping to stumble upon a stream or river. In the mornings, we licked blades of grass hoping to find some moisture. But it was pointless. We never should have left Illinois."

Agapito stands and squeezes Link's shoulder. "I am sorry that happened, Mr. Collie. It is hard to go on, but you must try to forget. You are young.

You must live your life. The dead will forgive you." Agapito speaks more emphatically than he normally does as he concludes, "Trust me." Agapito walks away from the campfire. As Agapito talked to Linc about the death of the young man's wife and child, I couldn't help thinking of Agapito's wife and baby girl. It was eerie. Though I never met Merced and Sarita, I felt like I could picture Agapito with them. If only Agapito could forgive himself. It's not Agapito's fault that Merced and Sarita were killed along the Santa Fe trail, either.

The Meek Man, as I think of the survivor, gratefully accepts the gift of an old dirty blanket, and takes several drinks of water before curling up beside the wagon master's campfire. He's asleep within minutes, and I whisper to the children to follow his example. Then, I follow Agapito to the edge of camp and stand beside him.

After a long silence, Agapito points to the west and says, "Do you see the sunset tonight, *querida*?"

"Yes." I turn my head and marvel at the brilliant colors. "It's glorious."

"When I see a sunset like this one, I think of change. It is like the leaves on the trees. Change is coming fast. It may not seem possible, but a week from now, people who have become like family will separate. We will say goodbye to old friends. Many, we will never see again. We will never forget this journey."

Saturday, October 12

It's a wonderful day along the trail. As we climb gradually into the Cascade Mountains, the terrain becomes greener and trees more plentiful. I love the wide open western spaces, and yet, at the same time, I miss the densely forested Adirondack Mountains we left behind last fall.

We're greeted by a cheerful man at Barlow Gate. He makes his way along the chain of wagons, introducing himself and collecting tolls. He vigorously pumps Stillman's hand. "I'm Chet Westerly. Sure am glad to see you all. It's been frightful lonely around here lately. You made it just in time. We're about to close for the season." Chet looks from Stillman to me and looks at us questioningly. It's as if he's thinking that Stillman's too young for me, or I'm too old for him. He greets Andrew and Christopher before kissing my hand and tickling my fingers with his thick mustache. When he does the same to Rose, she looks away but permits his greeting.

Chet says, "That's five dollars for the wagon and ten cents per beast. How many cattle, horses, and mules would you like to declare?"

Nearby, Dahlia Jane asks about donkeys.

"Yes, even donkeys must pay a dime to travel the Barlow Road. But, *little girls* may pass for free. In fact, there's no charge for any people."

"What about Dolly? Does she have to pay?"

Chet rubs his chin and his eyes narrow. "Nobody has ever asked me that before, but I bet lots of dollies have passed this way. I guess we'll let Dolly in for free. Does that sound good to you?"

"Yes, Mister. She's broke, and so am I." Dahlia Jane looks at Christopher. Boss sits patiently to the left of his master. She adds, "What about puppies?"

"Heavens to Betsy, yes. Puppies, kittens, dogs, and cats are free today. We're running a special."

"We don't have any kittens, but I wish we did."

"Oh, really? You might inquire at Philip Foster's Farm. You should reach there in a couple of days. Sometimes, they have kittens." With a jolt, Chet says, "Gosh, I better move along. We ain't got all day. Who is going to pay me? What's the tally?"

Stillman tells Chet how many of each type of animal we have. Alvah steps over from the wagon master's camp and says, "That's my wagon. I'll take care of the toll."

Before Chet steps away to collect Cobb's fee, he tells us to patronize his store. "Ain't much left, but maybe you can use some vittles. Cain't promise freshness, but if you ain't choosy, I can fix you up after I meet your neighbors."

When the gatekeeper is gone, Andrew says, "Phew! Thanks, Alvah. That's a hefty fee, wouldn't you say?"

Alvah sighs and says, "Imagine how much he charges for spoiled food." He shouts to Chet, and as he trots over to Cobb's wagon, Alvah asks how much it would cost to buy up all the store's provisions.

When the wagons are circled, fires are kindled, and axles are greased, I step over to the wagon master's camp and ask Alvah how much it cost him. Alvah doesn't answer, except to say, "He offered me a bargain price considering he's closing up shop for the season."

I look about and see bushels of apples and peaches, and at least a dozen loaves of bread. Alvah says, "That's not all we got, Dorcas. There's also a barrel of flour, a sack of sugar, and some coffee. How long would it take you to whip up some biscuits?"

Less than a minute after I set Alvah's skillet full of biscuit dough on the fire, Cian Reid follows his nose across the wagon circle. He looks lovingly at me, and says, "Sure, that's the finest thing I've ever had the pleasure of smelling, so it is."

Word circulates quickly, and soon a line of people forms at the wagon master's camp. The scouts pass out provisions to grateful travelers.

Cian stands next to Linc as Arikta passes by, passing out peaches. Cian says, "Ah, thank you kindly! You're an absolute gem, and I'm ever so grateful."

Cian and Linc devour their overripe peaches as if racing to finish. Juice drenches their chins, but they're so hungry that neither man cares. When they're done, Cobb asks them if he can have the pits. Maybe he can coax them to grow in his orchard.

When the biscuits are done, Cian looks at me with pleading eyes. I hand him the first one. He nibbles off a tiny bite and looks to the sky. "By the saints, this is the best biscuit I've had in ages. I'm ever so lucky to savor it." He walks away slowly as if entranced by the simple combination of ingredients.

By the time I've converted the last of the flour into biscuits, it's early evening. When I clean up, I hear a sound I haven't heard in a while. It begins as a plaintive wail, and becomes more exuberant. Before the song is over, a second fiddle joins the first, then a harmonica, and Jew's harp join the band.

I step toward The Hub and see our newest citizen, Linc Collie, talking with Berta's sister, Katrin. Seconds later a new song begins, and Berta steps forward, singing "Wayfaring Stranger" in German. Then she performs the song again in English. Oona Reid joins her for the second verse, harmonizing.

When the German and Irish women finish harmonizing, Bacon Bump begins to fiddle a lively tune. Agapito steps forward to call the square dance, and the frolicking emigrants tap into a reserve of energy after a toilsome week of travel.

My feet take me to the edge of camp. A large clone of quaking aspen flutters in the evening breeze. Brilliant yellow leaves contrast with the orange tinged clouds as the sun sets and the day comes to an end.

Yes, change is on the way, but we are eternally grateful for stale bread, wormy apples, overripe peaches, and warm biscuits.

Sunday, October 13

I'M QUIET IN THE morning. Many people sleep in, including the children. Andrew is the first to arise, and I remember sitting alone with him beside a small fire during the first days of our journey.

Andrew clears his throat, takes a breath, and says, "I've had a vision, Mama."

I close my eyes, as if bracing myself, and think, *what now*? "About the weather?"

"Well, bad weather is on the way, Mama."

Agapito, who is also awake, approaches our campfire.

Andrew frowns. I know he would rather speak to me confidentially than share his premonitions with others, though he might find others more willing to believe in such things. Despite the fact that he's often right, I can't help being skeptical, though I have come to rely on his weather prognostications. He continues, "There is a big storm on the way, but the vision I have is of a man, and his hands. I can see them lifting a board from a provision box, and a bunch of money underneath."

Agapito bends at the waist, and says, questioningly, "A false bottom in a provision box? That could be it. Do you think that someone is hiding Boss Wheel's fortune in the bottom of such a box?"

"I do. And that's not all. There's more. I have another vision of money being poured from a beat up old boot. A man's boot."

Agapito looks away from us and says, "Good Heavens." Those words sound funny when spoken by him. I can't help being amused, and I'm suddenly aware of the fact I say that phrase far too often. Now, Agapito has adopted it as well. "So, all we have to do is search the wagons, and we will find Boss Wheel's money?"

My son nods. "I guess." He frowns and says, "I don't know if I'm seeing Boss Wheel's money. And I can't be sure I'm seeing our wagons. But it could be."

Agapito scratches the back of his head. "People will not like it if we insist on searching their wagons, especially based on a hunch. Maybe I will say that somebody overheard a conversation." He flashes a smile at me and says, "It is true. When I came over this morning, I overheard a conversation between you and Andrew, *querida*. Never mind the fact that I joined the conversation."

The thought of the wagon master searching people's wagons concerns me. "People are protective of their belongings. There could be trouble. How will you go about it?"

"We could start with the most likely suspects. Then, we will not have to search many wagons."

"You could go in alphabetical order. Or, maybe you could use the wagon numbers."

Agapito grimaces. "That would be the most fair thing to do. But it would mean starting with Captain Meadows and The Committee. They are not going to like that."

"Yes, but if The Committee is searched first, it will be hard to claim favoritism later."

"You won't tell anybody it is my fault?"

"Yes. No, I will not tell. We will conduct an inspection and an investigation. Only, we will wait until the tired nomads are awake."

The search begins at noon. Agapito and the scouts spread out. Dembi Koofai stands near Landon Young's wagon, Arikta positions himself near Horace Blocker's wagon, and Agapito chooses a spot between Galusha Gains and Samuel Blocker's wagons.

When Alvah Nye tells Captain Meadows that he is conducting an investigation, raised voices begin to draw a crowd.

Captain Meadows recites the Fourth Amendment and argues against unreasonable searches and seizures.

Alvah reminds Captain Meadows that we are not in the States and therefore, the Bill of Rights does not apply. "Out here, we follow Boss Wheel's rules."

Captain Meadows stands aside and complains, "It's an insult!"

When Alvah empties Travis Latham's provision box, the man asks, "What are you looking for, anyway?"

Instead of answering, Alvah says, "I'm sorry to trouble you, friend."

The first three wagons are cleared. I'm not surprised. Who would have expected the Reverend or The Committee members to be harboring Boss Wheel's hoard of coins?

It doesn't take long for Alvah to inspect the Weavers, Carpenters, and Shaw's wagons. Alvah stops for a moment and says Leon Humphries and Clarkson Sawyer's names. Wagons number seven and eight no longer exist.

Sully Pierce grumbles but doesn't complain when Alvah searches his wagon. Alvah passes on searching Schuyler Steel's wagon. "I'll come back to this one last. There's no sense aggravating those bees if it isn't necessary." I can't help thinking that if I were trying to hide something, that would be the perfect wagon.

I'm relieved that Boss Wheel's money isn't found in the Lett's wagon. I couldn't imagine how Ross McAdams could have gotten away with the money, only to hide it among his in-laws' possessions, but who could know?

Horace Blocker complains about being treated like a criminal, but nothing is found in his wagon. The Reids and Appleyards don't put up a fuss, and Alvah searches their wagons quickly. In the interest of fairness, Alvah makes a point to search the wagon master's wagon and his own, although his wagon is technically number thirty-one. I can't help noticing that Alvah doesn't untie the covered goods at the front of his wagon, and I'm disappointed. I have a nagging curiosity about what lies hidden beneath blankets and twine in his wagon.

The crowd has grown to include Galusha Gains and Samuel Grosvenor, who protest loudly. Wayne and Bobby clutch their heads and appear confused. They look hungover. Is it possible the young men slept until noon? I thought their wives had poured out the last of their liquor. The whining sound of angry men grows as Alvah completes his search of the Banyons, Bumps, and Bulls wagons.

When Alvah makes his way to Bobby's wagon, the young man begs. "Please, mister. Don't." Bobby appeals to his friend. "They can't do this, can they, Wayne?"

Alvah says, "I'm sorry, friend." Aside from an empty liquor bottle, Alvah's search of Bobby's wagon comes up empty. Bobby grumbles when Alvah begins to search the exterior of his wagon.

When Alvah reaches Bobby's provision box, the young man crashes to his knees. With his elbows on the ground, the dark haired man rests his head on his forearm and groans. "I'm going to be sick. This can't be happening."

Just as Andrew had imagined, Alvah removes a board from the bottom of Bobby's provision box. Alvah leans the false bottom against the wagon wheel, and Serena gasps when Alvah removes a clump of bank notes and a mass of coins from the bottom of the wooden enclosure.

Wayne's forehead is covered in sweat and his eyes are wide. The man gulps and covers his chin with his fists as Alvah makes his way from Bobby's wagon. Drucilla turns her back away from Alvah, as if she can't bear to watch.

After a couple of minutes on board, Alvah emerges with a single boot. The way he carries it makes it seem heavy, like there is something within it. Alvah carefully sets the kicker on the ground, kneels beside it, and lifts his lip into a sneer as he pulls dirty socks from the boot's shaft. Then, just as Andrew imagined, Alvah pours gold and silver coins from the boot onto the ground. He looks up at Wayne, who squeezes his eyes shut. Alvah says, "What do you have to say for yourselves?"

Bobby stands beside his friend and hoarsely squeaks, "Undertaker's fee." He gulps and says, "We buried the outlaws. The ground was mighty hard to sink a shovel into and that money was just laying there, so we figured we could put it to good use."

Wayne nods in agreement. If there is a better excuse or explanation, he can't come up with one.

Galusha Gains laughs like it's the funniest thing he has ever heard of. "Boss Wheel's wife is going to be richer than the chief."

Horace Blocker shakes his head. "What a waste." Evidently, the man believes that the Brulé chief would not put the funds to as good a use as Bobby and Wayne.

Alvah searches the rest of the wagon train, but there isn't any more to be found. The mystery of Boss Wheel's fortune has been solved.

Captain Meadows grants Bobby and Wayne twenty dollars each as their 'undertaking fee' and places the remainder of Boss Wheel's estate in the hands of Agapito. Captain Meadows then pardons Bobby and Wayne for the crime of overcharging for funerary services.

Monday, October 14

This morning as we prepare for the day's journey, Arikta passes through camp with an ominous warning. "The road is steep. Do not walk behind the wagons. Stay to the side, and be prepared to step out of the way."

I look up the trail. After all we've been through, we've seen our share of steep roads and dangerous trails. Have the scouts forgotten that we're no longer greenhorns? And yet, I'm sure their warnings are necessary. I hope that my fellow travelers will heed them.

Arikta continues, "Carry blocks of wood, and if the wagon starts to pull backward, thrust the chocks behind the wheels."

The children look at each other and then at me.

Arikta tips his head forward and adds sternly, "This is serious. Last year, a runaway wagon killed three people. We do not want that to happen again this year."

"Say no more. We'll be ready. Thank you, Arikta."

ROLLING HOME

As the wagons depart from the campground at Gate Creek, Andrew clutches his stomach.

"Are you worried about the weather?"

"There's a storm coming, Mama. It's going to be a strong one. But that's not all. I think something bad is going to happen. All I can see is a messy brown jumble. And rocks. And trees. And wagons. I don't know, Mama. Oh, my head aches something fierce."

Yesterday, Andrew had a vision of finding Boss Wheel's fortune. It could have been left in the cave, but there was a really good chance somebody in our camp had it. It's hard to dismiss the hunch that the money was in somebody's provision box and an old boot as a lucky guess, but does that mean we should alarm everyone whenever Andrew has a bad feeling about something? Besides, what can we do but carry forth and finish our journey? The sooner we can get through the Cascade Mountains, the better.

Stillman and I take turns blocking the wagon wheels as Christopher drives the oxen up the steepest grade we've encountered yet. As poorly as Andrew feels, I'd like to tell him to ride in the wagon with Dahlia Jane, but it's all the cattle can do to keep the wagon moving forward. The trail is so steep, I can't help imagining that the wagons will topple backwards and roll all the way back to Tygh Creek. As I squat to set a block behind the wagon wheel, I chide myself for having an overactive imagination.

After a long day, we reach the top and the trail levels off. I look back to the east and the view is spectacular. White oak, maples, and aspens thrill the eyes with a kaleidoscope of color. Mount Hood stands tall above us, no longer far away, and I must tilt my head back to see the top. I can't look at the mountain without thinking of Horace Blocker and his fear of volcanic eruptions. I should check on him.

Andrew doubles over in pain and falls to his knees, groaning. I wish that I could do something to help ease his pain. I step to Rose's side and ask if she has anything to help settle Andrew's stomach. She answers, "When we get to camp, I'll make him a tea. That should help."

I glance back at the trail behind us. It feels like we have climbed all the way to Heaven, only who would take a prairie schooner? If it weren't for Andrew's suffering, the feeling of having made it to the top of the world would be much more rewarding. After we ford the White River, the wagons circle for the evening at Barlow Creek. I look up at Mount Hood, gleaming above us. It feels like we've made camp in a famous landscape painting.

When I carry an empty pail to the river, a voice shushes me, and I realize that I have been humming "Wayfaring Stranger," the song Berta and Oona sang the other night. It's Horace's son, Adam. I stop fast and halt my humming as he pulls a foot long, speckled trout from the creek. I raise my arms and wave my fists in a silent cheer. Hooray for Adam!

I make my way to the stream, leave my pail at the edge, and step from stone to stone to cross it. When I reach Adam's side, I'm surprised to see that the fish he just caught is the smallest of three. I look at him, amazed, and say, "How can such big fish live in such a small river?"

"I don't know. Maybe they're from a bigger river, and they found their way here." I compliment his fishing skills, and he tells me it is his favorite thing to do, but usually he gets skunked. The fish always seem to get the better of him. He concludes, "Maybe my luck has changed."

I smile, lean toward him, and say, "I believe it has."

"Would you like to try, Mrs. Moon?"

"Sure. I'd like that very much"

He fishes a grub from his pocket, baits the hook, and passes his pole to me. "Why don't we move a little bit upriver?"

When we reach a spot that Adam likes, he points to a dark pool and wiggles his finger. I don't know if fish can hear voices from the riverside, or whether it's a matter of superstition, but I don't say a word as I dangle the grub on a hook into the water, slowly letting the line loose and sinking the hook to the bottom of the pool.

From out of nowhere, a fish makes a surprisingly violent hit on the hook, and I jump.

Adam compliments my skill, setting the hook, and I thank him rather than tell him that I had been startled. As I pull the flopping fish from the water and let it splash among the sedges, Adam leaps on it, removes the hook, and bashes its head with a rock. "You must be quick, Mrs. Moon. Otherwise, they'll flop back into the river."

I hand the pole back to Adam. I should return to camp, fill the water barrel, and gather wood for tonight's campfire. Instead, I sit back and relax, watching the boy drag a dozen trout from the river. We've been hungry for a long time. That boy's going to be a hero as people eat their fill of trout tonight.

Tuesday, October 15

Andrew predicted bad weather, and it has been raining since dawn. Instead of letting the weather halt our progress, most of us move faster instead.

The dreaded Laurel Hill is the steepest downward slope and, according to the crew, the most dangerous obstacle along The Oregon Trail, unless you count rafting up the raging, Columbia River, but we did not go that way. To prevent our wagons from careening down the steep hill, we must cut down heavy trees to drag along behind the wagons. Some use saws, and others chop down trees with axes.

Woodchips fly as I crack my blade into the truck of a spruce tree approximately forty feet tall, and ten inches in diameter. As I chop, I look down the steep hill we've dreaded for months. From the corner of my eye, I notice movement and hear an unexpected sound. What in the dickens is going on?

"Hi-yah!" Horace Blocker shouts and snaps his whip over the back of his oxen. It's unusual to see somebody drive oxen from the back of a wagon. The man who ordinarily doesn't go anywhere in a hurry can't seem to move his wagon fast enough to suit him. What is he doing? We're not ready to descend Laurel Hill, and Horace most certainly isn't prepared. That fool plans on driving over the edge without dragging an anchor behind him.

Horace is too far away for me to do anything to help. I don't know what difference it would make if I were closer. What could I do? It is too late to stop or prevent what is about to happen. The axe falls from my hand. The tree I'm chopping down will have to wait to be felled.

It's a hard thing to have to watch a disaster unfold before one's eyes. I could look away. After all I've witnessed this past year, I wouldn't have thought that anything could surprise me. Mad as Horace has become, why should I be shocked now? I step forward slowly as the Blocker family's wagon pours from the lip of the mile-long hill's summit. As I stand at the edge of the precipice, I concede that what we've been told is true. Laurel Hill *is* the worst we've seen yet, and we've hauled our cargo over many steep hillsides.

The wagon is only thirty yards along, and already, it is going way too fast. "Why didn't he chain the wheels first?" Who do I think I'm talking to? Everyone else is far afield, chopping down trees of their own. "Why didn't he wait?" A thousand whys can't change what's happening now.

Two hundred yards farther along, Horace's wheels spin so quickly, the spokes can no longer be seen. The chasm followed by the trail narrows. There's scarcely room for a wagon to pass through the channel.

I should cover my eyes, but for some reason, I can't seem to do it. I feel myself leaning forward as if compelled to compensate for Laurel Hill's steep decline by leaning in the opposite direction. Horace's wagon is moving way too fast.

I can't tell whether it's because of rocks or the slippery path, but I can feel my cheeks twist into a grimace as Horace's wagon swings from side to side. The man is thrown from the wagon and pitched forward. There's no way he can avoid being crushed beneath the rig as it tumbles forward. It may be just my imagination, but I am sure that I can hear him screaming.

"Oh! Oh, no." I can't shake my disbelief away as, one after another, the oxen trample their master. Then, the heavy wagon's wheels roll over the man, causing it to tilt. The left wheels follow the deep rut, worn into the hillside, and the right wheels are lifted from the channel over Horace's body, pitching the wagon to the left. The wagon moves faster and faster, too fast for the oxen to manage. They can't outpace the force of gravity and they stumble as the wooden vehicle crashes into them from behind, crushing them beneath the rubble.

Horace Blocker didn't even make it halfway down the slope. The wreckage sticks to the trail for a long second before skittering down the hillside, like an avalanche. It reminds me of watching the destruction of our wagon in the Grand Ronde River. Moments later, nothing is left of the man, his wagon, or his family's belongings.

Alvah Nye shouts as he runs toward me. When he reaches my side, he is breathing heavily. He implores, "Dorcas, what happened?"

I rub my eyes and shiver. The real question isn't what happened, but rather, why? I turn toward our leader and shrug. "I wish I knew. What possessed him to set off down the hill, by himself, unprepared?" My head shakes, pitifully. "We should have known better than to leave him alone. He went mad weeks ago, and I knew it, Alvah. But, I never knew he'd do *this*."

"It's not your fault, Dorcas. What could you do? When a man takes a notion to do something stupid, he usually can't be stopped."

Hours later, Alvah, the scouts, and a dozen men work to clear the debris from the bottom of the narrow trail. The steady rain becomes a miserable downpour. One by one, our remaining wagons tentatively enter the channel, brakes locked, wheels chained, dragging forty foot tall trees with their branches intact. Men argue with Alvah Nye, insisting that we stop and wait for the weather to improve. He insists that we move faster.

When the last wagon makes it to the bottom, I look back up the trail. It doesn't look like any dirt remains. Whatever soil there was on the steep mountainside looks like it got flushed away in a mudslide.

When we make camp in the rain, a few miles beyond the horrific hillside, I try to console Horace's widow. Adam tells his sobbing mother, "Good thing I had my fishing pole with me." He looks down at his feet and says, "But I lost a shoe coming down the mountain. Now what do I do?"

Instead of responding, Lana wails louder.

I try to reassure Adam. "Try not to worry, son."

With my arm over Lana's shoulder, I say to the woman, "Why don't you join me in the wagon? Adam can bunk under the awning with Andrew and Christopher." I don't mention the scouts who also shelter beneath the canvas.

The rain shows no sign of letting up. Adam will have to grow up fast, just like my boys. All the kid ever wanted to do was go fishing. Somehow, he'll have to get along and make do.

Agapito says that the nearby stream is named Zigzag Creek. It looks more like a raging river. Except for Horace Blocker, we have survived the notorious Laurel Hill, but will we make it out of the Cascade Mountains with the rivers flooding?

WEDNESDAY, OCTOBER 16

IN THE MORNING, ANDREW says that the weather will not let up today. He goes on to say, "Tomorrow looks bad too," but smiles as if the foul weather is a good thing.

I inquire, "Why do you look so happy?"

Andrew pats his belly. "I don't have a stomach ache, Mama." He knocks his head with the base of his hand. "And my head doesn't hurt neither." He makes a goofy face, and says, "I can't think of any aches or pains, whatsoever. How about that?" He whispers, "Do you think that means we're home free? No more trouble ahead? Wouldn't that be a blessing, Mama?"

With a nod and smile, I concur. "We can suffer the weather, just as long as there are no more tragedies. It's time for our luck to change."

He blinks and looks lost. "Luck?"

I shrug. "Would you rather say, good fortune instead of luck?"

"I don't know. It sounds so haphazard. Is everything just happenstance? Good luck? Misfortune? What about destiny? How about God's plans for us?"

I rub Andrew's back, and say, "I like to think we have a lot to do with what happens to us. We never know what others will do, or dangers around the corner, but how we face our challenges accounts for a lot too, wouldn't you say so?"

Andrew nods and the wind kicks up. He says, "Did I mention that the weather will not let up today?"

I laugh and take our place in the chain of wagons.

As we march, I marvel at the raging rivers. They remind me of springtime in the distant Adirondack mountains, which we left behind last year. But it is not spring. This is autumn, and it seems very different from the pleasant days we often had before winter began, back east. What a misfortune to travel in such miserable weather.

As the wagons stretch out along the trail, I walk beside Lana Blocker. Just ahead, Andrew, Christopher, and Adam trudge along, practically huddled together. It's as if my boys are trying to shield Adam from the soaking rain. If only the Grand Ronde River hadn't wrecked our wagon. It would be a comfort to don that India rubber rain gear now, but that's lost along the trail, like so many other useful possessions.

In a strong voice, Lana says, "It was kind of Mrs. Appleyard to give Adam those moccasins." Normally, the woman speaks quietly, almost in a whisper.

Her acknowledgment makes me feel even more sympathetic. "Charlotte is very kind, and quite a seamstress as well. She's also a skilled nurse." I reflect for a moment on how much she means to me. I've come to treasure my friendship with the kind woman from Virginia.

We travel along quietly for a while. I imagine that Lana must be thinking about her family's tragic change of fortune. We're silent for so long that I'm almost surprised when she speaks. "Horace is gone. I should be sad, but I'm not. Don't tell Adam." Maybe it's because of the heavy rain that she projects her voice.

Rose appears beside Lana so suddenly, both Lana and I are surprised. Rose's shoulders hunch forward and I can't help thinking of Horace, who walked with a similar posture. I cringe to see the heavy rain dripping from Rose's wet head and worry that she'll catch a chill.

In a plaintive tone, Rose says, "Lana, I'm sorry about what I did. How I lived. I never found what I was meant to do. Or, who I was meant to be. If I had only given something a chance instead of finding fault in everything. Different. Things would be different. The boy needs friends. People. Adam should not be alone all the time, or he will end up like me." When Rose is done talking, her body straightens out, and she sweeps rain from her stringy hair with her hands. Then she eases away.

Lana looks at me, and I can see the disbelief on her face. When we look back, Rose is gone. I turn and see her climbing into the back of the wagon master's moving wagon.

Our wagon train's newest widow practically shouts at me. "I can't believe it."

She shelters her chin in her elbow, and then releases it. The tone of her voice conveys a sense of rapture. "It's remarkable. It's as if your daughter were possessed. I think Horace took over Rose's body. I never imagined seeing anything like that." Her body noticeably quakes. "You saw it too, didn't you, Dorcas?" The cold, wet rain could explain a shiver, but I'm sure her twitching comes from thinking about spirits. "Please, don't tell me I'm imagining things. I must be losing my mind."

I try to make excuses. "You must forgive Rose. Sometimes she behaves strangely. It comes and goes, but the last year has been difficult. She says the strangest things. She doesn't intend to be rude, and she's not trying to be funny. She's just trying to help, in her own way."

Lana leans forward and shouts, "But Dorcas, that's just it. She *did* help. It sounded just like Horace, speaking to me. Only usually, Horace wouldn't say more than a sentence at a time. Your daughter has a gift. A very rare gift. Those things that she said were just what I needed to hear. If only Horace could have said them to me when he was still alive." She looks downward at her hands, one clasped in the other. Sadly, she concludes, "Perhaps things would have been different."

Hours later when we make camp just beyond the crossing of the Sandy River, I overhear the boys talking. I don't listen long, but hear Adam tell Andrew and Christopher, "He may not have been much, but... I don't know. I feel like he understood me and let me do what I wanted."

Christopher says, "Why don't you come with us when we get to Oregon? We can be neighbors. Maybe you could live next door."

I turn away from the children and step toward the wagon. What if Lana and Adam came with us instead of following Galusha Gains and Samuel

Grosvenor? Why not? I think of fishing with Adam a couple of days ago and I can't help smiling to myself in the rain. My stomach grumbles and I can't remember having eaten anything today. My mouth waters at the thought of fresh caught, pan seared trout.

If only we could have another fish fry now.

Thursday, October 17

Just as Andrew predicted, soaking rain continues as we break camp. It rained all night, as it did yesterday, and the unrelenting precipitation sometimes eases to a steady, light rain while we march, but never stops completely. Most of the day, it rains heavily and soaks us thoroughly. Could this be the aftermath of a Pacific typhoon? Are monsoons common in Oregon?

The scouts ride from wagon to wagon, warning us. Arikta says, "Do not stray from the trail today. Sometimes, we lose wagons over the edge."

Dembi Koofai nods once and looks serious, as always.

Arikta continues, "Follow the wagons rather than walking wide to the side. The rain makes it worse, and we do not want anybody to slide off of the ridge. This is called the Devil's Backbone for a reason."

Smoke and oakum, why must they have such dramatic names for the horrifying segments of this trail?

Dembi Koofai brings his hands together, and the slope of his arms conveys the danger of steep mountainsides. Perhaps it is the Indian hand sign for the word *ridge*. In my head, I hear a blatting sound, and think of Ridge, the milking goat we have on loan to Cobb. I think of the goat's spine and a hogback as overlapping images.

The trail becomes more treacherous as we go. Three times, we must slow our procession and ease the wagons over the steepest parts of the trail by securing rope around strong tree trunks, and lowering the wagons carefully to gentler sloping terrain. It's hard not to think of Horace Blocker's suicidal descent of Laurel Hill, or the day poor Leander Bull was crushed by a wagon near the summit of Rocky Ridge, way back in June.

One time, while we wait for a wagon to be winched over the edge, one of Cobb's Devons stumbles. I can't help but scream as I watch it careen over the edge and tumble to its death. Cattle, and Devons in particular, are normally well centered and surefooted. My body tenses. Water flings from the brim of my hat as I shake my head in denial. I wish I hadn't seen that happen. I recall the grizzly bear that killed another one of Cobb's yearlings. How many kine remain from Cobb's initial herd?

Mercifully, the heavy rain obliterates our view, sometimes. But mostly, the high, waterlogged clouds allow just enough visibility to see over the edge of the steep embankments so that we can make out the narrow ridge ahead. I'm not typically worried about heights, but the narrow trail and slippery footing make the declivity terrifying, and Cobb's bull is a grim reminder of what could happen.

When the trail is at its narrowest point, Rose steps toward me and walks beside me for a minute before speaking. She says, "We're with child, Mama. I told Charlotte, and she confirmed it, but *we* didn't need the doctor and his wife in order to know."

I tip my head forward and breath fast. I say, "Oh, Rose," and she interrupts me.

"We know her. She has shared her soul with us." Rose says *she* reverently, as if the pronoun were her name and the unborn child were a deity. "She has not yet decided if she wants to stay and live a life. It will be hard for her. She understands that. Maybe she needs to live a challenging life. When she knows for sure, she will let us know."

I can feel my eyes tighten. Hopefully, Rose cannot see the grimace on my face. Though I don't put enough stock in prayers, ever since Snarling Wolf was killed I have often looked toward the Heavens with the hope that Rose had not conceived a child during their marriage.

To make matters worse, it is a challenge to never let on how I feel about the disturbing things she says. What a load of rubbish to think that an unborn baby can conceive thoughts and make life or death decisions. And what about this *we* and *us* language that Rose uses? It's as if she thinks that she's speaking for herself and Snarling Wolf. I feel a tingle along my shin, and imagine a wave of goosebumps traveling up my leg.

I gulp hard. Good Heavens. Of course, when one's child has a baby, one becomes a grandparent. I blink and realize that in all the time I have worried about Rose becoming pregnant, I never thought about that. If I hadn't felt old before, the idea of becoming a granny is an undeniable sign of aging. I tell myself that I'm only thirty-four, but it doesn't help.

When I look at Rose, she's smiling, though she isn't looking at me. It isn't often that she appears happy. She doesn't seem to notice the cold rain that drenches us. Her face makes slight movements, a flicker of the lips and a twitch of the brow. It is as if she's having a conversation with someone.

Then she turns to me and says, "Snarling Wolf says not to worry. You will make a wonderful granny, even if you don't believe in spirits."

I turn my head away from Rose for a few steps. Of all things! To think, Rose would have me believe that the dead can know the thoughts of the living and pass messages back and forth. Holy smoke!

When Rose begins speaking again, I turn to face her as she says, "In early spring, I'm leaving Oregon, and returning to Washakie's village."

"But honey, you can't travel alone through the wilderness. What about late winter storms? How will you find your way? No, it is not practical."

"Don't be worried, Mama. We'll be alright. Snarling Wolf will show me the way and protect us from harm."

I groan. How can I argue with this sort of logic? I say, "We'll see."

Rose sternly says, "No, Mama. Not, *we'll see*. I know what's best for me, my baby, and my family. We do not belong in Oregon. The plains and prairies are our home."

There's no convincing a stubborn teenager who has made up their mind about something, even when their decisions are ill-conceived, or foolhardy. I don't say another word. Instead, I shall hope that reason will catch up with her before she embarks on a disastrous journey.

When we reach camp for the night, Agapito tells me that the turbulent fury we're camped along is Tickle Creek. I drop to a squat and cover my face with my hands. I laugh like a mad woman. If I were to see me right now, I'd think myself crazy, but I can't help it. I'm surrounded by madness. Usually, I think of myself as the only sane one, but it feels like my belly will split open as I laugh so hard my face hurts, and my ribs feel like they're about to crack.

Tickle Creek? Goodness gracious!

When I finally regain my composure, I stand, look up at the clouds, and see a growing patch of blue sky. I feel a hand at my waist and an arm around the small of my back.

Andrew says, "Don't worry, Mama." His voice cracks, and for a second, it sounds deeper before returning to its regular pitch. "The storms have passed. We'll have good weather now."

Agapito steps to my side and says, "This is Oregon, *querida*. You have made it." The family gathers around, facing west.

I think back to the time we had our family portrait taken in our home town last year. The daguerreotypist told us to stand perfectly still, and then he preserved our images forever onto photographic paper. If only we could take our picture now, looking out over the Willamette Valley, aside the wild Tickle River. I'd prefer to have a bath and new clothes before recording our appearance for the sake of posterity, but maybe we'd be proud to preserve an image of how we looked as travel hardened frontier stock instead of showing off our Sunday best.

Friday, October 18

After a short day's travel, we catch a peek of civilization. First, on the horizon, we glimpse a faint tendril of smoke. As we get closer, it appears as a thick, twisting column, rising from an unseen source. Finally, we can smell it. It doesn't just carry the familiar scent of a campfire but also the warm, heady fragrance of dishes not tasted for far too long. Our hungry stomachs remind us that we've endured short rations for a very long time.

The view is ablaze in color. Expansive oak trees spread orange and yellow foliage across the landscape. The vibrant autumn colors contrast with the bright, azure sky and verdant evergreens. Quaking aspens and mature grasses add movement to the scene.

We gasp in unison at the bucolic view, dominated by an ample farmhouse. Along the way, we've seen forts and cabins, but it's hard to remember seeing such a lavish structure. Aside from the freshly built barracks at Fort Laramie, all of the structures we've seen since have been crude and utilitarian. Philip Foster's farmhouse looks like the home of a wealthy, country town's leading citizen.

It takes a couple of minutes of staring at it to take the whole scene in. The homestead features a sizable barn, several outbuildings, sheds, and structures, and even the outhouse looks as big as our wagons. The terrain is lush, though it is mid-October. Despite the fall color, harvest is neither complete in the gardens nor the fields.

I look back at Cobb beside the wagon behind me. As always, he has Jenny cradled in one arm and the bullwhip in his other hand. I point at Philip Foster's orchard, and he nods vigorously and points at it as well, the length of the whip extending the reach of his gesture. I think of his wife's dream of sitting in the shade of an apple tree, sewing, in Cobb's orchard. Have the saplings that Cobb has nurtured all the way from New York survived? Perhaps. We will have to wait until spring to know for sure.

When the wagons circle near Eagle Creek, I step toward the center of the ring for a moment. Soon, many of us will go back to being strangers. I watch as Cian drops to his knees and digs into the ground with his bare hands. As he pulls fertile black soil from the earth and lifts it into the sky, I imagine him eating the stuff. We're all famished. After smelling the rich dirt and letting it drop through his fingers to the ground, I know exactly what he's thinking. Potatoes. He shouts, triumphantly, "I can make something of this."

Most of us are too excited, and hungry, to spend much time getting ready to patronize the farmer's hospitality, but I insist that the children wash their faces and comb their hair with the mane comb. I gather the flighty mess of my hair into a bundle on my head and wish I had time to take a proper bath before stepping back into the civilized world, but there's no time for such vainglorious notions.

Our hosts warn us as they feed us at tables outdoors, family style, not to eat too much or too quickly. They tell us a story about children gorging themselves on sweet, juicy peaches, eating so many, so fast, they ate themselves to death. As I dip a spoon into a mountain of mashed potatoes, I look over at Cian, and see a twinkle in his eye as he scrapes his plate. The children slather butter on bread, and make the sounds one makes when they taste something delicious. Dahlia Jane points at a delicately iced cake and tugs on my sleeve. Whether or not the story about gormandizing to the point of dying is true, most of us leave the best meal we've had in months, stuffed to the gills.

After dinner, I accompany Alvah and Agapito as they show the homesteader the outlaws' stolen cattle, horses, and mules, offering him first choice. I can tell that Alvah is about to accept Philip's first offer. The prices are low, and I'm sure many arriving emigrants have animals to sell, but we can't let the herd go so cheap. Before thinking twice, I say, "We're going to need to get a better price than that, Mr. Foster."

He turns back to Alvah and says, "I could go five percent higher." He stretches out the phrase, "I suppose," as if our asking him to pay more is unreasonable, especially after the hospitality he extended.

Before Alvah can respond, I say, "Twenty percent higher would be a fair price, I would say, Mr. Foster."

Philip rubs his hand roughly across his face and groans. He counters with fifteen percent.

I say, "I think we'd better have twenty percent, Mr. Foster."

It's clear to see his jaws tense as he frowns. "Fine, I'll pay your price, but you must take a quarter of it in store credits."

Alvah says, "You have a deal."

Still frowning, the farmer slaps Alvah's shoulder, and says, "No fair, letting a lady dicker the price. Who could say *no*? I've been bamboozled." It would seem that his outlook has rebounded quickly, and his hearty laughter contrasts with his spoken words. I'm sure we would have spent at least a quarter of the money on trade goods anyhow. By the time we part company with Mr. Foster, he's referred us to buyers for the other half of the outlaw's herd.

When we distribute the proceeds from the sale of our ill-gotten gains, everyone is delighted. The money is allocated equally, counting every man, woman, and child, and most travelers received twice what they paid for passage along the trail. And still, we have only sold half of the stock.

Several families pay $3 to spend the night in one of Philip Foster's cabins. What a luxury, to spend a night under the protection of a roof, and surrounded by firm walls, all the way from a wooden floor to a leak-proof ceiling. But, for that price, clean bedding and stuffed mattresses should be included. What would Larkin think if I spent money so frivolously? I must admit, thinking of him now makes me smile. Six months ago, I might have spent the $3 just to get his goat, but he was right to be frugal. I will only spend money on things that we need, or investments that can pay us back.

At the farm stand, I purchase a butter churn, two bushels of potatoes, a fat, broody hen, five pullets, and a crate of assorted fruit. I would have bought clothes for the family, but Agapito whispers, "You will save money if you buy clothing in Oregon City." I've spent far less than a quarter of my share of the money, but expect that other families will make up for it by spending more. Agapito extends his arm and pulls me closer. He says, "One more day of travel, and we will reach our destination. The end of the trail. Our journey's end."

I say, "We should just stay here. This is the Oregon I have imagined."

Before we leave the store, Agapito whispers in my ear. I think of Chet Westerly at Barlow's Gate, look at Dahlia Jane, and nod assent. He picks her up and carries her toward Philip Foster's barn as I help Stillman, Andrew, and Christopher carry our purchases back to the wagons.

Saturday, October 19

It's hard to be grateful sometimes.

I recall Chet Westerly at Barlow Gate telling us to inquire about kittens at Foster's Farm. It was nice of Agapito to make sure that we didn't forget. After all that Dahlia Jane has been through, often forgotten or overlooked along the grueling trip, it's good that her dream of having a cat has come true, but I must have been crazy to permit it. She chose the cutest little cream-colored creature I've ever seen, but the little monster is all claws and fangs, and howls like a wounded animal when caged. How can I let the child hold such a ferocious beast? The more the kitten screams, the worse my head aches. It is a challenge not to screech, myself, from frustration.

After yearning to arrive in Oregon City for so long, it is hard to look at the tattered buildings, muddy streets, and disorganized settlement with admiration. It's not even better than Independence, the town from which we departed, half a year ago. Oregon City is situated in a long, narrow canyon, along the Willamette River. There are stores, shops, and hotels, each with a crude sign, and many are painted in drippy letters, with misspelled words. I guess I don't care about spelling anyhow, it's just that when a place has been so widely praised, one expects it to be idyllic. Philip Foster's farm was the land of milk and honey, but the end of the trail, plainly, is not.

We meet Sarah Terwilliger at Abernethy Green. How many times have we heard and uttered the rallying cry, "Do it for Sarah! Sarah Terwilliger!" Her brother and sister, Landon Young and Grace Weaver, are kind and friendly, so I always imagined their sister would be welcoming. Maybe the loss of her husband last year soured her disposition. It can't have been easy to live as a widow in a strange, new land, and depend on the kindness of friends and fellow travelers to support her young children. When she greets her siblings with a sharp tongue and a sour face, I turn around and walk away.

My first priority is new shoes and clothing for everyone. I round up the children and herd them off to the cobbler's shop. I'm glad to have Lana and Adam join us, as well as Cobb, Bess, Joe, and Jenny. If it weren't for the windfall provided by the sale of the outlaw's stolen stock, I wouldn't be able to outfit the family, and I know that my fellow travelers wouldn't either. After doling out five dollars per pair, I sigh, happy to have proper shoes on the children's feet.

As we're preparing to leave, Cobb asks the cobbler where we should file our homestead claims. The man answers his question with his head turned up, and I listen intently to him. When he's finished, he seems to relish saying, "But *you* can't file a claim."

I interrupt. "What do you mean he can't file a claim? Why not?"

The man indignantly explains the so-called black exclusion laws, and then tells me that me and my husband, on the other hand, can file for 640 acres. When I tell him that my husband has died, he says, "I'm sorry," and shrugs, "but you can't file a claim either. Just single men or married couples."

My chest deflates. I look at Cobb and his head hangs so low that his chin almost touches his chest. He looks like he might drop Jenny. I take the infant from him and wonder whether there is also a Mexican exclusion law. I decide that we've had enough information for one day, and nudge Cobb and the children toward the doorway.

Our visit to the cobbler's shop was not pleasant, but at least we have shoes. I should have negotiated with the proprietor. Perhaps we could have saved a couple of dollars. At least there's no sign in the window forbidding Cobb from entering the shop, like there was at the store in Independence.

On the way to the next store, I shake Cobb's elbow and tell him not to worry. "We'll figure something out, you'll see."

He frowns at me and says, "I should have known better than to believe things would be different in Oregon." When I promise him that we'll see to his place, with plenty of room for his orchard and cattle, his mood doesn't improve. He mutters, "What's the use? Things will *never* change."

I shake my head at the sign that reads *cloths* instead of *clothes*. The shop's proprietor doesn't look into our eyes as she listens to our requests, and directs us toward the clothing that meets our needs. I almost wonder whether the woman is blind. Perhaps she's leery about getting too familiar with strangers, or maybe she's disdainful of emigrants. I pick a plain, solid, pink dress, and a set of clothes just like the ones I inherited from Larkin, to wear underneath. That shall have to do. I pick equally ordinary, but properly fitting clothes for the children, and resolve to be miserly with our remaining funds. If I cannot file for free land, I shall have to purchase some.

When we return to the circled wagons, I hear my old friend, Esther, complaining. She says, "Is this it? After all these months and miles, *this* is our *just reward*? This wretched place is not fit for swine."

I'm not near enough to Esther to have to respond or rebut her complaint. She's probably not the only one to feel as she does. After all we've been through, someone should throw a parade celebrating our long awaited arrival. We should be welcomed as heroes. Who cares about Oregon City anyway? We didn't come all of this way to live in a town.

Esther yelps, and then howls. She shouts, "A bee just bit my caboose. That Schuyler Steele, I'd like to wring his neck. What was he thinking, dragging those wretched insects all the way from one end of the country to the other?"

I step away, hoping to distance myself from Esther's complaints. It's been ages since we've spoken to one another. I should be sad that we've grown apart, but at the moment, it's hard to remember what I ever liked about her to begin with. One shouldn't have to be friends with somebody merely because they hail from the same place.

Sunday, October 20

After twenty-four hours of being surrounded by so-called civilization, I feel crowded. I can't catch my breath. It's like I'm trapped in a place so small, I can't move around. I think of a coffin, and grin wickedly. How quickly can we get out of town? Maybe we should just leave today. Now that we've arrived in Oregon, we no longer need to follow Captain Meadows' rules. Who cares if it *is* Sunday? Not me.

I reflect on Reverend Meadow's Sunday services. He was in rare form today. I wonder if he spent most of the last six months planning the words he would say when we arrived. It's as if the man expects us all to follow him to the town he plans to found. I thought we already settled where everyone was going. To me, it sounded like the man planned to run for Governor of Oregon. Maybe someday, Oregon will go from being a territory to statehood. Perhaps they'll need a man like Captain Meadows to preside over it.

I think of those who plan to follow Captain Meadows, and I don't feel sad about parting ways with them. I feel a little guilty for not being sad about separating from Addie and Esther, but the one person I would like to bring with us is Luella, the gentle soul who enjoys cutting people's hair, despite her powerful husband's mild objection to it.

Leaving friends and family behind, I wander along the riverside, ambling southward. Thoughts dart in and out of my mind. One after another, like paintings in an artist's studio, I see images from along The Oregon Trail in my mind, and wonder if they will fade as the years go by.

How long has it been since I've thought about Noah? For so long, I wondered whether I would ever get over him. When he disappeared for years, I waited for him to return, but he stayed away too long. After three years of waiting, I married Larkin. Noah never loved me anyway. Maybe he thought he did, but when he came back to town, and married Arminda, I felt betrayed, though it was me who married first. The fact that Larkin was Noah's best friend made it worse. After all those years of being married to Larkin, I still pined for Noah. But somewhere along The Oregon Trail, I let him go. I correct myself. I let go of both Noah and Larkin.

I fill my lungs with crisp, autumn air, and watch the current in the Willamette River. I let them go, but when? Was it the day I stood on top of Independence Rock, with my legs spread wide, hands on my hips, leaning forward into the wind? Perhaps it was the day I stood looking into the mirror after discarding Larkin's safe at the Red Buttes of the North Platte River. I close my eyes and remember how it felt when Agapito stepped up behind me, and I saw an image of us together in the looking glass. Maybe it was the day I roped the wild mustang, Gwibunzi, and felt like I belonged in the wilderness, wild and free, like her. My eyes mist and I blink quickly, in a flutter.

How is it possible that I have found the answer to all my questions here, along this river at the end of the trail, in a place where I do not intend to remain? Maybe I didn't know it at the time, but I got over Noah the moment I heard that musical voice on the muddy street in Independence. That was even before I ever saw the man from whom it came. It was not love at first sight, but perhaps a love that was always meant to be—a love that had to wait its turn. Though I'd hate to admit it to anyone other than myself, I got over Larkin that same day.

For half a year, the fates have conspired to keep us apart. I couldn't take up with the Mexican assistant wagon master while I was still married. Boss Wheel's rules always hung over us like a dark cloud, and Agapito's promise to Merced made me realize that it was impossible for me and Agapito to ever be together. I convinced myself that I would remain a woman alone. That wouldn't be a bad fate, and if it weren't for Agapito, it could suited me well. Then, the man almost died. Maybe he did die. When he came back to life, I think I knew then, I can't be a woman alone. Not as long as Agapito lives. I belong at his side.

I gaze to the east, and gather my frayed hair into a bundle, poking unruly tresses into place. My memory of the day before our journey began, when Agapito held shooting lessons outside of Independence, and we talked about our dreams, replays in my mind. I remember practically every word we said that day, and have thought about the wisdom of Agapito's words many times.

A thrill shoots through me. The dream that has long eluded me couldn't be clearer to me than it is right now.

I want to breed and sell horses. Philip Foster crosses my mind, and it occurs to me that I increased the price of our transaction relatively easily. I'd like to be a rancher, and I've changed my mind about love. I'll be as happy to live Agapito's dream as my own. I remember him saying that loving somebody means that you try to make their dreams come true. I told him that I'd follow him back and forth between Independence and Oregon City each year. Maybe he didn't fully hear or understand me. I told him that I didn't care if he married me, that I would live as his woman anyhow. I don't need a home to be happy. A rolling home would suit me fine. The children would have to adapt. I don't know how we would get on with a puppy and kitten along the trail, but we would find a way.

For a moment, I think about Lucky Nye, the man who wanted a woman who would slip beneath his blankets in the middle of the night, but found conversing with a woman difficult. I obliged myself the fantasy of imagining slipping beneath Lucky's blankets, but never followed through. When Lucky kissed me, I pictured Agapito.

Now, I see the man of my dreams in my mind, naked as a wild animal in the dim light beside the river. If we hadn't been interrupted, what might have happened then? It thrills me to think about it. I would not have hesitated. Whatever the consequences, I was prepared to meet them. If only Stillman and Dembi Koofai had not interrupted us.

Why hasn't Agapito mentioned that night since? Why hasn't he brought up my proposition? Must I tell him again? What if, now that we have arrived in Oregon, he rides away in the middle of the night? He wouldn't abandon Arikta, or Boss Wheel's business, would he? He promised that he would take us to the perfect homestead site.

A feeling of dread overwhelms me. What if tonight is our last chance to be together?

Monday, October 21

It's past midnight, and I should be fast asleep. My heart pumps as excitement surges through my veins. At the same time, fear of rejection looms over me. I know we have a long travel day planned for tomorrow, but I'm not going to think of that now.

I stand in the borrowed wagon, and my head feels funny. I sit for a second, until the dizziness passes, and then climb carefully from the wagon, as quietly as I can. There's only one person I want to awaken. The last thing I need to do is step on Lana Blocker.

As I tiptoe toward the wagon master's camp, I wonder whether a sinful creature such as myself should disrobe before she slips beneath a man's blankets or wait until she's there to wriggle from the confinement of her garments. Then, I worry, what if somebody else is sleeping in the bed in the back of the wagon master's rig?

While Agapito was recovering from his injury, he slept in the wagon, but maybe he no longer does. Imagine how embarrassing it would be if I accidentally nestled into Alvah, or one of the scouts, instead of Agapito. Daunted by the prospect of an unintended surprise, I warily climb aboard and shuffle quietly to avoid tripping. My eyes blink rapidly in the darkness and my heart drops. The blankets are mussed, but there's nobody in the bed. Where is Agapito?

My thoughts race as I lower myself slowly to the ground. I peer at the sleeping lumps beneath the wagon master's canvas awning. It's hard to guess who is where. Wary as scouts are, I'm sure to awaken them if I get too close. I turn away from camp and wander into the darkness. Disappointed, I realize that I shall have to give up on my plan. After a brief stroll, I'll return to the wagon and try to fall asleep.

When I reach the horses, I'm surprised to see him. He says, "What are you doing here, *querida*?"

I gulp. "Looking for you. What are you doing here?"

"I have watch tonight. Remember, I told you that."

I don't have the slightest recollection of him telling me that, but I don't want to waste any time or lose my resolve. I step forward, wrap my arms around him, and pull him close to me. Our lips meet. I kiss him, tenderly, savoring the moment, and then I pull my head away, slowly, so I can look into his eyes. I say, "I do know my dream now, and I've changed my mind about love. I'll marry the first man who asks me. If he does not ask me to marry him, I will slip beneath his blankets in the middle of the night."

The corner of his mouth turns slightly upward, and I can see amusement in his eyes if not the dimples at the corners of his mouth. He says, "This is good to know. I shall keep this important information in mind. We should talk about the future, but I would like to do that tomorrow night, not tonight. I have watch, and you should get some rest before dawn. I must tell you that Captain Meadows also has watch tonight." He kisses me delicately, and then releases me. "Tomorrow, after we make camp, let us go for a walk, and we can talk then."

I lean forward and kiss him once more. "Tomorrow, then." My body tingles all over. I fight the urge to touch his face.

Agapito puts his hands together beside his face and pretends to rest his head on an imaginary pillow. His voice quavers as he says, "Sweet dreams, *querida*."

On the way back to the wagon, my mind races. How in the world will I fall asleep now?

Today, our destination is eighteen miles in the distance.

Agapito says that he wants to show me a pristine valley. It's a couple of miles south of Philip Foster's Farm, on the east bank of the Clackamas River. Agapito says its grassy hillsides, ancient forests, and spectacular views will make my heart soar. The nearer we get, the faster my heart beats. A year of travel has led to this moment. This country truly is the land of milk and honey. I imagine rolling down the hill like a child, and hugging the ground when I reach the bottom.

Instead of circling the wagons, our remaining prairie schooners form a square near the riverbank. Our new, small village includes: Bobby and Serena Bond; Wayne and Drucilla Horton; Hollis and Charlotte Appleyard, as well as Violet and Pious Bull, Jr; Berta and Ross McAdams, and the Lett family, as well as our tag along, Linc Collie; Charlie Banyon and his children; Cian, Oona, and Aengus Reid; Lana and Adam Blocker; Alvah Nye; Schuyler Steele, who changed his mind at the last minute; the wagon master's crew; and my family, including Stillman Southmaid.

When we finish an early supper, Agapito asks if we can take a walk together.

Stillman looks at me, raises his eyebrows, and says, "Go on, Dorcas. Don't worry. We'll be fine." A smile widens across his face, and I glance at Agapito, who shrugs and looks about like he doesn't know what Stillman is thinking. Whatever Agapito plans to say to me, I can see that Stillman already knows.

Rose rolls her eyes. It reminds me of when she called me a dorbug and a dolt. She has the same look on her face now. It is as if she knows something that I do not. I say to Agapito, "Very well."

As I begin to stand, Agapito extends his arm. I take his hand and follow his lead into a lush meadow along an irregular line of enormous trees.

As we stroll, I say, "This land is gorgeous. It is so bountiful. I can just imagine horses grazing in the meadows, and there is plenty of wood and water. Looming large above it all, there is the supreme, frosted cone of Mount Hood."

"You are not afraid of the volcano, are you? Hopefully, she is at peace now."

"Yes, she has quite a history, but I think she is content now."

"Yes, she does." Agapito turns, steps toward me and draws me close. "She has quite a history." His face inches toward mine, and he looks deeply into my eyes. In a low voice, he asks, "Do you think you could be happy here?"

I nod my head very slowly. "You were right about this spot. I'm so happy you brought us here." It is true. I could be happy here, but I'm not certain. If I had my choice, I might prefer the high plains.

Agapito says, "I am glad, *mi amor.*"

Not *estimada*, nor *querida* either; that's a new phrase I haven't heard before. "Those are pretty words. What do they mean?"

"My love. I have been waiting for the perfect time to say it. Now that we are alone, and the moon is full, I know there will never be a better time than now. Dorcas Moon, will you marry me?"

Goosebumps slide down the back of my neck, and I feel light-headed. I stand frozen like an icicle as Agapito's expression changes from earnest to amused. Though my eyes are locked onto him, I'm acutely aware of the heavenly setting that surrounds us. I let another couple of seconds tick by and wish that this moment could last forever before I place my hands gently on his back and pull him toward me. My bosom presses against his chest, and I feel a wave of desire stronger than anything I have ever experienced with a man. I kiss his lips gently, ever so briefly. Then I gaze into his antelope eyes, turn my head slightly, and say, "Maybe."

There's a mirthful twinkle in Agapito's eyes. The dimples at the corners of his mouth become more pronounced as a grin spreads across his face. His eyebrows dance as he says, "Oh, I see how it is. I thought you said that you would marry the first man that asked you. Must I prove my love to you now? Shall I scale the volcano, slay a dragon, or conquer an empire to win your heart?"

"Oh my goodness. Heavens, no." My spirit soars as I gush, "But I have a question."

"What would you like to know, *mi amor*?"

"Once, you told me that when you love someone, you try to make their dreams come true. Then, you said that you were in between dreams."

"You have an excellent memory, yes? Can you believe that was a half a year ago? I am no longer in between dreams, *mi amor*."

"A lot has changed, hasn't it?"

"Yes, many things have happened."

"Six months on the trail is like a whole lifetime. There is much death, many tragedies, but excitement and adventure too."

"I am always sad when the journey ends and we must say goodbye to people who have become like family. This year, I am not sad."

"But what about your new dream?"

His long slender fingers gently caress my cheeks. He says, "When I joined Boss Wheel, I thought my dream was to be needed. But you have made me see that my true desire is to be loved. I wanted to be with you when we first met, but as the months went by, I only wanted you more every day. When you brought me back to life, and stayed by my side while I healed, I knew you loved me too. The bullet hole in my chest has healed, and now, the hole in my heart has been filled as well."

"What about Merced?"

He wistfully turns his head. After a moment, he says, "She was right. She told me *not* to keep my final promise to her. Merced was smarter than me. Perhaps she knew that you would come along. I will always love her, and I know you loved Larkin too."

I say, "Perhaps they are watching over us." Movement in the sky distracts us, and we watch a pair of chickadees flit along. I'm reminded of the lovebirds we saw at Scots Bluff. I look back at Agapito and say, "I've changed my mind."

"Oh, have you?"

"Yes." I press my cheek against Agapito's and gaze off toward Mount Hood. "Not maybe. The answer is yes. I *will* marry you."

Agapito blinks rapidly, and tears pool in his eyes as he presses his lips against mine. "You have filled my heart with joy."

I close my eyes, and he kisses me deeply. His passion overwhelms me. His long tongue engages my own in a dance, twisting and twining recklessly. He leaves me breathless, desperate to fill my lungs, then we go back for more. I never knew that a kiss could feel like this.

Lacking air, I pull away and ask, "When? When can we be married? I don't think I can wait to be together, my love."

"Then we should marry tonight."

"How is that possible?"

"When there is no captain, the wagon master can perform a wedding."

"Can you preside over a wedding and be the groom?"

"No."

"It was a good thought, Agapito." I feel my heart sinking. "We shall have to wait a little longer, then."

"No. I quit my job. The assistant wagon master is now in charge. Would you mind if Alvah Nye marries us?"

Instead of answering, I wrap my arms around him and smother him with a kiss of my own.

On the way back to the wagons, I ask him whether he's ready for a large family. He says, "I love your children, *mi amor*."

"All of them?"

"Yes, I love all of your children."

"I've got *a lot* of children." He nods reassuringly as I say their names: "Rose, Andrew, Christopher, Dahlia Jane, Stillman, and Ross, The Cherub."

"You forgot a couple, *mi amor*."

"I did?"

"Yes, do not forget Arikta, and Dembi Koofai."

"Yes, of course. How could I forget about them? Let's tell them the good news!" I reach for Agapito's hand and we hurry back.

A flash of color catches my eye as I spy a strange object in the distance on the way back to the wagon. I gasp as we step faster toward camp. Everyone has gathered behind the beautiful new cookstove that I discarded at Red Buttes with Larkin's safe.

Words fail me. All I can say is, "How?"

Agapito chuckles. "Alvah Nye travels lightly. When you were distracted, they tied up your stove and stowed it in Alvah's wagon."

I'm amazed. "It's been there ever since the North Platte?" I look from one person to another. My gaze rests on Dembi Koofai, and he turns his body sideways as if he's trying to disappear. I say, "And you knew?"

Dembi Koofai confirms with a hand sign as the rest of the crowd verbalizes. Evidently, everyone knew but me.

Agapito says, "If you would still like to marry me, now would be a good time, *mi amor*."

I turn my head and think for a moment. Agapito is wearing his best clothes. I look back and say, "I have a new dress. Would you give me a few minutes to put it on?"

Gallantly, he says, "But of course."

I hotfoot it to the wagon, climb aboard, and disrobe. The crisp, pale dress is a little loose, but not as much as the one I've worn for the past six months. I hold up the old dress. It has been through so much. It is the frock that walked The Oregon Trail. It's tattered, torn, stained, and threadbare, but it made it, all the way from Independence to the land of milk and honey.

In my haste, I forget to don the shirt and trousers that I wear beneath my dress. I realize my mistake as I step from the wagon and decide not to correct it.

Excitement shoots through my body as I make my way through the gathered crowd. I can't wait to get to Agapito's side, yet I step as slowly as I can. Why rush this moment? I want to remember it forever.

As I approach, I'm overwhelmed by how gallant he looks. He appears serious as a soldier, but there is a mischievous look on his face. Our eyes are locked on one another, and yet he holds his chin high, his shoulders pitch back, and his chest juts forward. He watches me intently, and as I draw nearer, his lips part. He briefly places a hand over his heart, and then he takes my hands in his.

The newly promoted wagon master stands before Agapito and the crowd, holding a Bible, and waits. It dawns on me in a rush. This is really happening. Dreams do come true. It is possible to be with the man I love, and love can come at any time.

There are tears in Alvah Nye's eyes as he says the final words that join us in matrimony. The crowd sighs as we kiss.

Agapito whispers, "I have always dreamed of finding a woman I could look up to. But I never expected my dream to come true."

We are interrupted by a loud honking sound. As we turn to face the crowd, Charlotte blows her nose again. After she pockets her handkerchief, Hollis reaches an arm around behind her and draws her to his side. Next to them, Violet and PBJ hold hands and smile. Berta stands in front of Ross, and he rests his hands on her shoulders. Oona leans into Cian and rests her head on his arm.

I glance from face to face at those who've traveled all the way to Oregon with us, and decided to remain together now that we are here. Arikta nods at me. Dembi Koofai, who seldom wears a shirt, sports a crisp clean tunic I don't remember seeing before. Instead of looking at me from the corner of his eyes, he stands facing us with a hint of a crooked smile on his face. When I look at Bobby, he punches Wayne in the arm and they laugh.

Nearby, Stillman raises his arms in the air and shouts, "Hip, hip, hooray." Next to him, Dahlia Jane jumps up and down, screeching, gripping her dolly tightly in her hand. Christopher holds Boss tightly against his chest and covers the puppy's ears with a hand. Andrew holds a notebook at his side. Our eyes meet and he winks at me. Rose's fingers fiddle with the choker that Snarling Wolf gave her. She tilts her head, turns slightly, and looks off into the distance.

When the crowd grows quiet, Agapito says, "Me and my wife are going on a short trip. We will be back in the morning." He picks up a stack of blankets from the top of a barrel and tucks them under his left arm. His right hand reaches for mine. As we return into the hills, he says to me, "It could get noisy and bumpy, so we should be alone."

I can't help laughing. "You were listening that day. I knew it. You snoop!"

Tuesday, October 22

In the morning, on our way back to the wagons, hand in hand, Agapito says, "Rose asked me to take her to Washakie's village in the spring. She said she is going, whether I take her or not, but that you will be happier if she does not make the trip alone. I told her, with your permission, that I will go with her."

"I'm not ready to let her go, Agapito. Maybe I never will be."

He tips his head forward and says, "I understand." Maybe he'd like to say more than that, but I'm not sure if I want to hear it.

I stop and tug Agapito to a standstill. He turns to face me. "I don't know if you do, Agapito. You see, I dream of a ranch, not a farm. I want to raise horses and sell them. To travelers. To the army. Whoever needs them. I'm not sure about Oregon. It's not just Rose who feels this way. I might prefer the plains and prairies, also. I haven't thought about it enough. Anyway, my plan was to go with you, back and forth between Independence and Oregon City. Not settle down."

Agapito says, "I do not care where we live. Either way, you can be a rancher. You can decide in the spring, but we need to build a cabin. It will be a very long winter without shelter."

I place my hand on his chest. We can talk about that later. I need to tell him about the deadline for filing a Donation Land Claim by the first of December. "And another thing, Agapito. If we stay, I want to give Cobb half of our land. If we go, he can have all 640 acres. Do you mind? He's worked as hard as we have, wouldn't you say?"

"I do not mind. You have a big heart, *mi amor*."

We finish our short trip to camp and the smell of breakfast makes my mouth water. When I see four mounted riders, I drop Agapito's hand and clutch my stomach. Who could eat now? Breathing becomes hard, and I must force myself to inhale.

My pleading eyes meet Agapito's. He says, "They must make their way back to Independence to meet next year's passengers."

"How will they get there? Should we change our plans and go back with them, after all?" He looks at them and back at me. From the look on his face, I imagine he's thinking that we shouldn't hold them up. I tuck my chin to my chest, as if I might hide my eyes, and then realize that I'm not wearing my hat. I whimper, "I didn't know that they planned to leave straight away."

"They will journey south to California, and make their way east, across the desert. It is many miles, and they will need to move at a steady pace."

My eyes fill with tears, and I turn away from Agapito. It has been clear to me for a long time that Alvah Nye was meant to be a wagon master, or some sort of guide, but I will miss him terribly. With my back to my husband, I ask why they're not taking a wagon, and he tells me it is easier to buy a new one in Independence than to be slowed down by it on the way back.

I turn back to Agapito and wonder. It must be hard for him also. He has been like a father to Arikta, and perhaps Dembi Koofai also. He's not just parting with friends, but a way of life that he has lived for a very long time.

My voice squeaks as I shout at the young men. "Climb down from those horses at once." I throw my arms around the strapping bear of a man. "I'm going to miss you, Alvah Nye." After hugging the Pawnee scout, I can't help kissing his cheeks. I feel bad for taking Arikta's father figure from him. Embracing Dembi Koofai is like hugging a tree. Has anyone ever held him in their arms? Quietly, I say, "I've grown mighty fond of you, my friend. Thank you for..." it is hard to settle on one thing to mention, "everything."

Saying goodbye to the fourth young man makes my heart ache. I sob as I pull Stillman close. My hand finds the back of his head and I pull him to my chest. I don't care if I'm smothering him. I can't help myself. "I've told you this before, but I couldn't love you more if you were my son. I'm proud of you, and grateful for everything—your love, friendship, and assistance at every step of this journey. I don't know if we could have made it all the way here without you, Stillman. You're a fine man, and I wish you a world full of happiness. You deserve it." I squeeze his cheeks together and he looks like he's about ten years old. I kiss him on his cheek and let him go. As I wipe tears my tears away, I say, "You owe me a letter, Stillman. Promise you'll write."

As Stillman climbs back into the saddle, I realize that he's riding Rio. I look at Agapito and my hand covers my mouth. He steps forward to my side and says, "She will serve him well. Rio knows every inch of the trail. Stillman could not ask for a better companion."

I blink rapidly, and proudly say, "What a handsome outfit you make." I wish that I could paint a picture of the four men on their mounts, Alvah on the big bay, Arikta on the striking black and white paint, Dembi Koofai on the black Appaloosa, and Stillman sitting proudly on Rio, the golden buckskin.

One at a time, the riders turn their horses and trot away to the south. Dembi Koofai is the last to turn. Before he does, he raises his hand and makes the sign for *friend*. I imagine a tear at the corner of his eye. Perhaps it is not a figment of my imagination. I guess I shall never know for sure.

I smile and return the gesture. Even now, as he rides away, that young man makes me wonder. What has he been through? He's steady, strong, and silent, but there's something about him that remains a mystery. There's a deep hurt that troubles his soul. I wish I could have helped him.

Rose says, "You did, Mama. You helped him, more than you can know. You helped all of them."

Andrew says, "They'll be fine, Mama. You'll see."

Dahlia Jane says, "They didn't say goodbye to Boss and Paw." It's the first time I've heard the kitten's name. Did she name the cat after Larkin?

Christopher sniffles and I turn my head toward him. He struggles not to cry. The cream colored cat sits calmly in his hands. Somehow, he has tamed the wild creature already. He says. "I want to go with them, Mama." His jaw clenches, but tears form in his eyes. A couple of seconds pass before he adds, "Someday, I will." I know it's hard for a boy his age to be separated from his hero. Children hate to be told that they're not old enough. Though he acts much older most of the time, he isn't even ten yet.

Rose nods reassuringly. She says, "Time may pass, but we will see our friends again."

You've endured the hardship, disasters, and challenges of a massive migration. It's been a pleasure having you along for the journey of a lifetime. Thank you for reading *Rolling Home* and the Ghosts Along the Oregon Trail series.

How about another rollicking adventure?

It's 1868. Grab your hat, step into your boots, and strap on those spurs. Your cow pony is saddled up and ready to ride the Chisholm Trail.

A brand-new cattle ranch drives its first herd to market. The trail is fraught with hazards from perilous river crossings to the mother of all stampedes. When the drovers realize that they're being tracked, followed, and hunted, a growing sense of doom overwhelms the fledgling outfit of wet-behind-the-ears cowboys.

Since they left San Antonio, the drovers have looked forward to whooping it up at the end of the trail. That was before somebody began killing cowboys. Now, Abilene seems like an impossible dream.

Will anybody make it to the end of the trail? Order *First Drive* today!

If you want to get your first look at this new adventure, claim your free copy of *Farewell to Poesta Creek*, a prequel novella.

ANOTHER JOURNEY

You've reached the end of the trail. Let's partner up for another exciting expedition. Get ready for a rollicking cattle drive adventure in 1868.

Order *First Drive* today. Snap the QR code and follow the trail to the author's website for more information.

About the Author

David Fitz-Gerald writes westerns and historical fiction. He is the author of twelve books, including the brand-new series, Ghosts Along the Oregon Trail set in 1850. He's a multiple Laramie Award, first place, best in category winner; a Blue Ribbon Chanticleerian; a member of Western Writers of America; and a member of the Historical Novel Society.

Alpine landscapes and flashy horses always catch Dave's eye and turn his head. He is also an Adirondack 46-er, which means that he has hiked to the summit of the range's highest peaks. As a mountaineer, he's happiest at an elevation of over four thousand feet above sea level.

Dave is a lifelong fan of western fiction, landscapes, movies, and music. It should be no surprise that Dave delights in placing memorable characters on treacherous trails, mountain tops, and on the backs of wild horses.

A Tip of the Hat

This series is affectionately dedicated to the countless authors whose words have preserved the legend of the Oregon Trail, the diligent historians who have meticulously chronicled its history, and the brave emigrants who embarked on a perilous journey in pursuit of lofty dreams. Additionally, this series pays tribute to the indigenous peoples whose ancestors lived, loved, and died in these lands since ancient times. The rugged peaks and fruited plains, simultaneously abundant and inhospitable, bore witness to their stories. May their tales always echo through the canyons of history, preserving the spirit and honoring the legacy of those who walked the path before planes, trains, and automobiles.

Thank you to the collaborators that helped me bring Ghosts Along the Oregon Trail to life: editors Kolton Fitz-Gerald and Lindsay Fitzgerald; singer songwriter Kyle Hughes; White Rabbit Arts at the Historical Fiction Company; and the coaches at Author Ad School.

Deep gratitude to my Facebook group, Adirondack Spirit Guides. I appreciate the guidance, support, and early reader feedback. A special nod to Gail Cook, who was the first to make it through the series.

This project also pays homage to a genre that I've loved as long as I can remember. The old west in fiction, history books, landscape paintings, movies, television and songs inspired this project. If you think a character name is similar to an iconic western hero, you're not mistaken. Some of the characters' names were pulled from the roots of my family tree. For example, a woman named Dorcas is my 6th great-grandaunt. Many monikers are plucked from film credits. The unusual character, Fritz Franzwa is named to honor the work of a dedicated historian who researched, documented, and published *The Oregon Trail Revisited* and *Maps of the Oregon Trail*, which helped me cast my fictional emigrants on an incredible trail.

During my research for this project, I had the opportunity to visit many of the Oregon Trail's landmarks. It could take a lifetime to visit them all, but I'm well on my way. I've had the pleasure of crisscrossing the historic trail on the scenic byways in Wyoming and Nebraska, and I recall a sweltering day during a record-breaking heatwave in the 1980s. My brother, Jeff, and I visited the mostly abandoned town of Jeffrey City, Wyoming, which boasted a population of three. It's situated near the Oregon Trail and the Sweetwater River. We purchased soft drinks, but by the time we made it back to the truck, the red cans had already gone warm. It was *that* hot. The truck wasn't air conditioned, and I remember sympathizing with the pioneers, trudging along beside a chain of wagons. More recently, I had the pleasure of visiting the National Frontier Trails Museum in Independence, Missouri; the Fort Bridger State Historic Site; and the White Mountain Petroglyphs. It's off the trail, but I just had to send my characters there.

I'm *most* grateful to *you* for stepping away from the present, into the distant past with me. Thank you. I'd love to hear from you. If you get a chance to drop me an email at dave@itsoag.com, I'd love to know: if you were alive in 1850, would you have chosen to follow the Oregon Trail?

Made in the USA
Monee, IL
01 August 2024